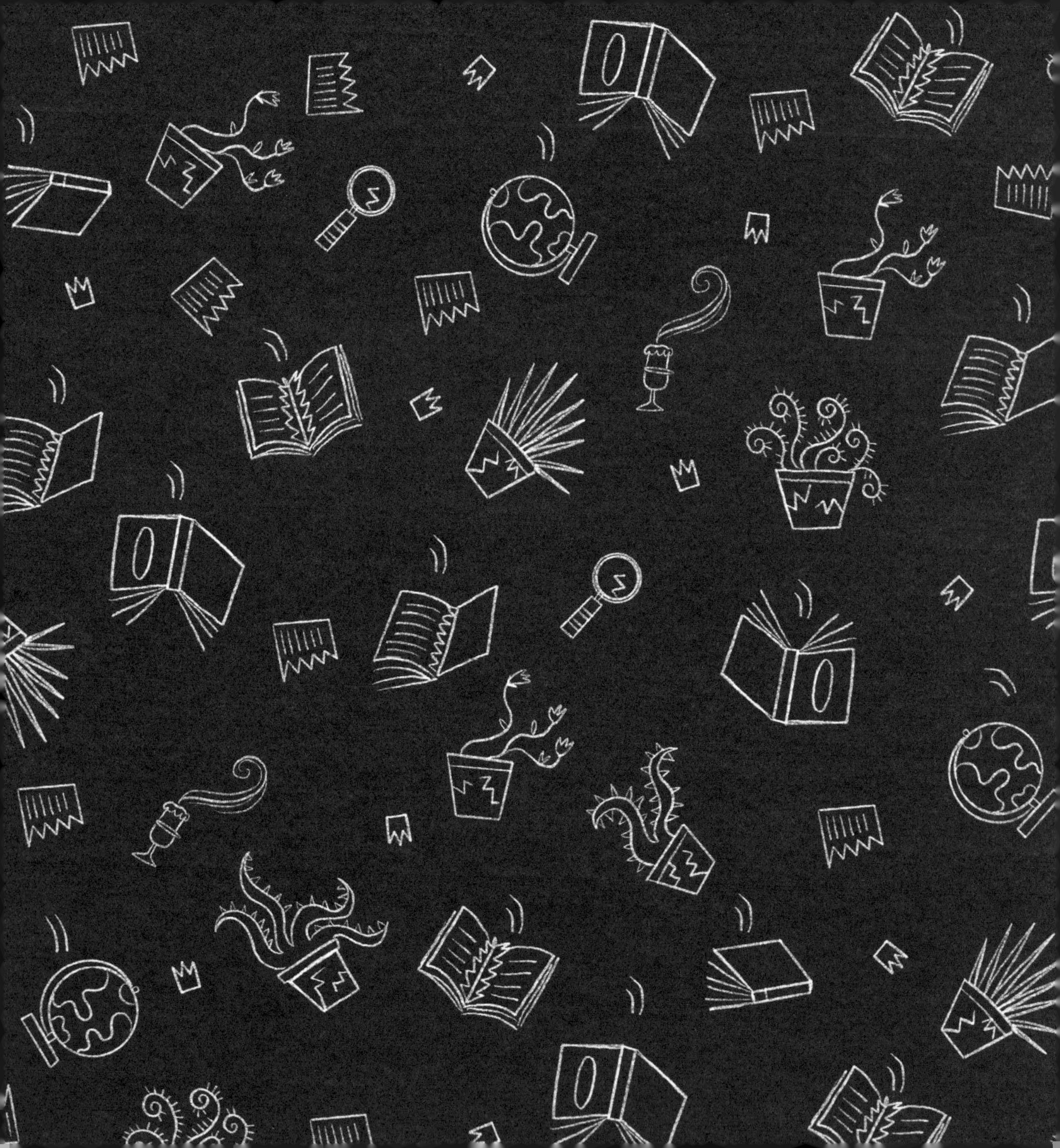

for William from
Great Gramma Bailey

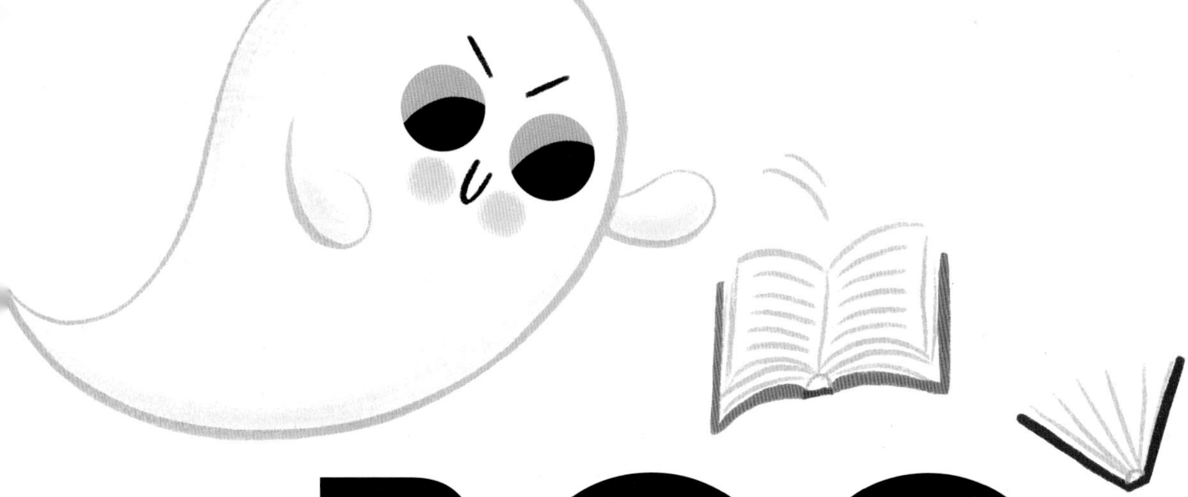

BOO
the library ghost

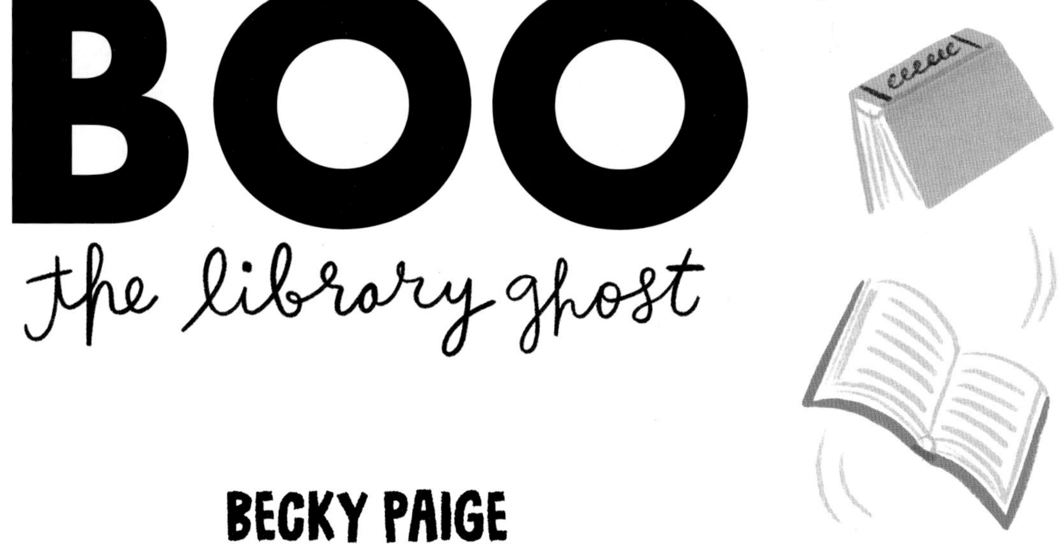

BECKY PAIGE

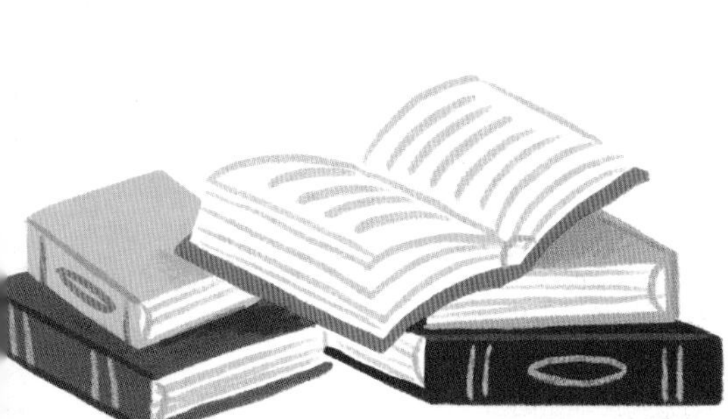

Silver Dolphin

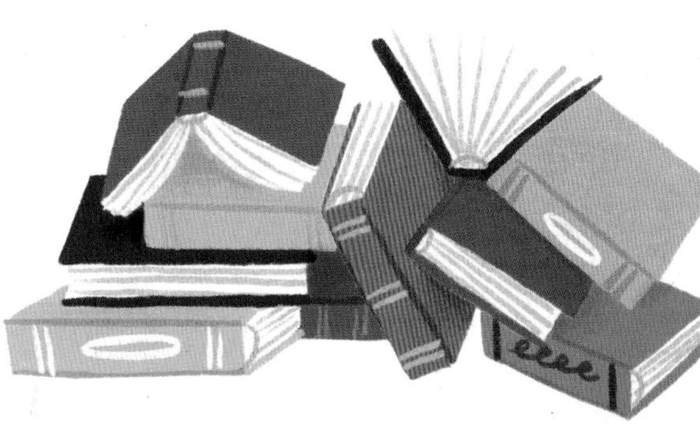

Silver Dolphin Books
An imprint of Printers Row Publishing Group
A division of Readerlink Distribution Services, LLC
9717 Pacific Heights Blvd, San Diego, CA 92121
www.silverdolphinbooks.com

Printers Row Publishing Group is a division of Readerlink Distribution Services, LLC.
Silver Dolphin Books is a registered trademark of Readerlink Distribution Services, LLC.

ISBN: 978 1 6672-0688-2
Manufactured, printed, and assembled in Heshan, China.
First printing, March 2024. LP/03/24
28 27 26 25 24 1 2 3 4 5

The library is haunted!
Beware of the ghost!
Frightening children
is what Boo loves to do most.

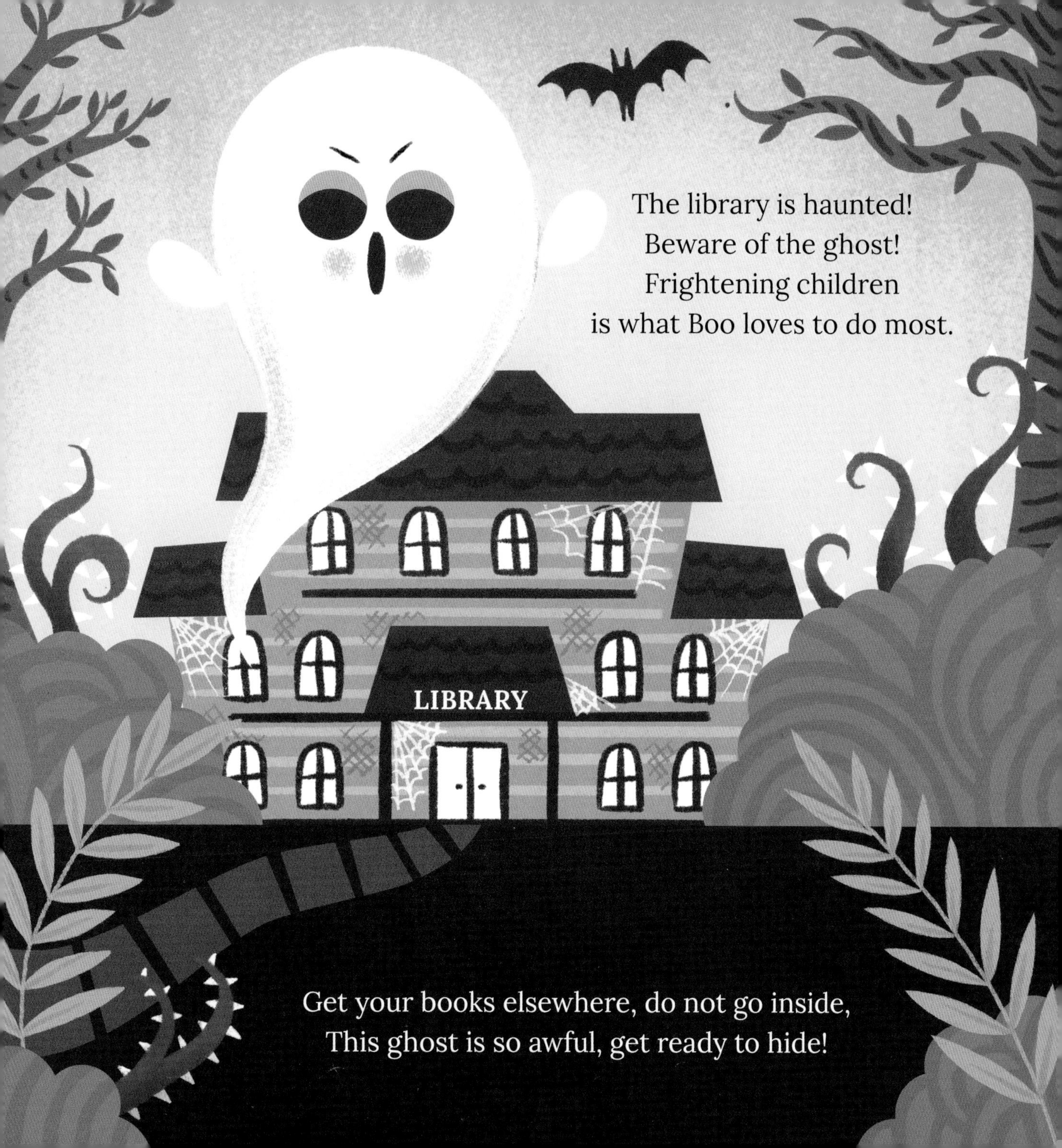
LIBRARY

Get your books elsewhere, do not go inside,
This ghost is so awful, get ready to hide!

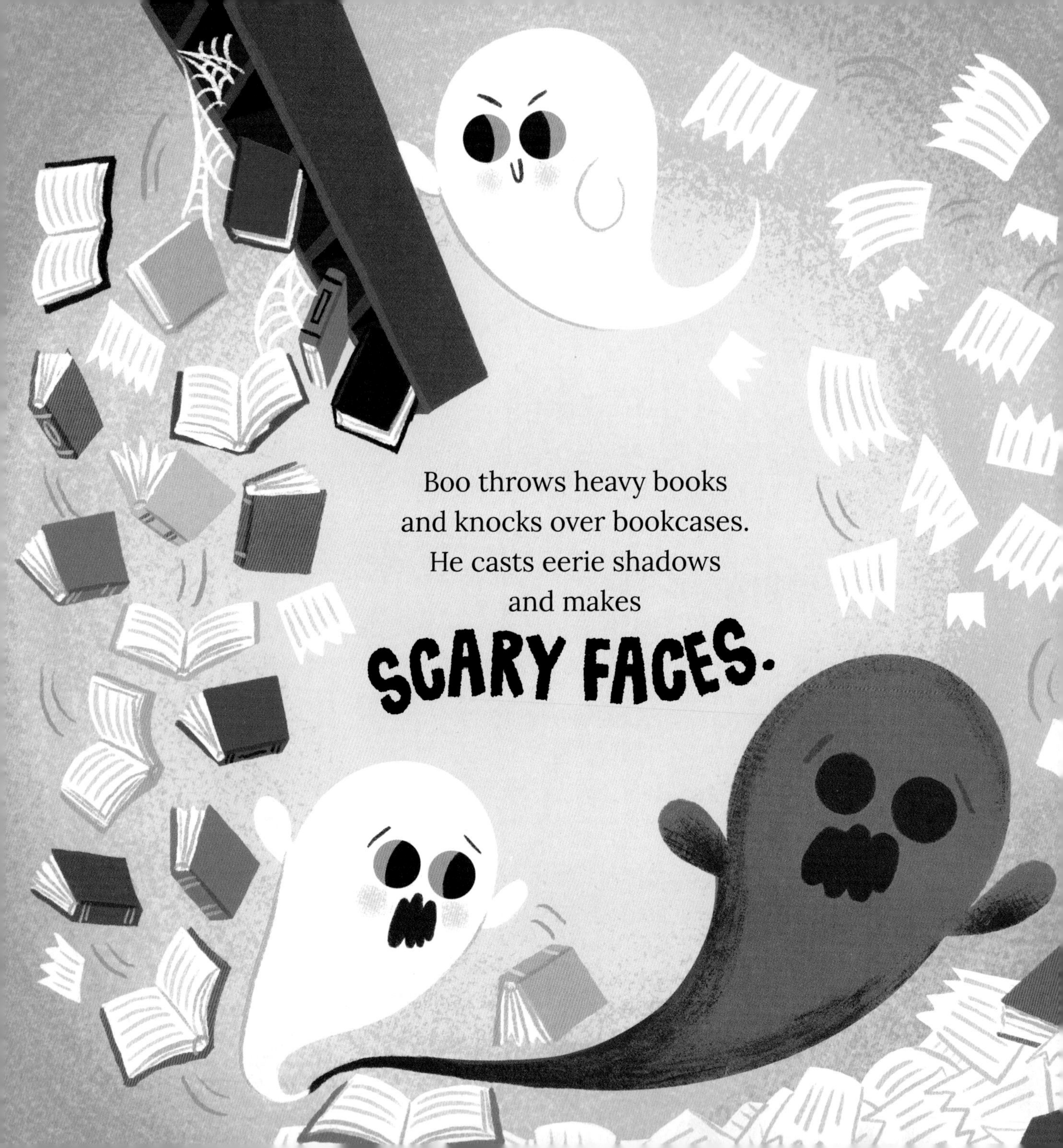

Boo throws heavy books
and knocks over bookcases.
He casts eerie shadows
and makes

SCARY FACES.

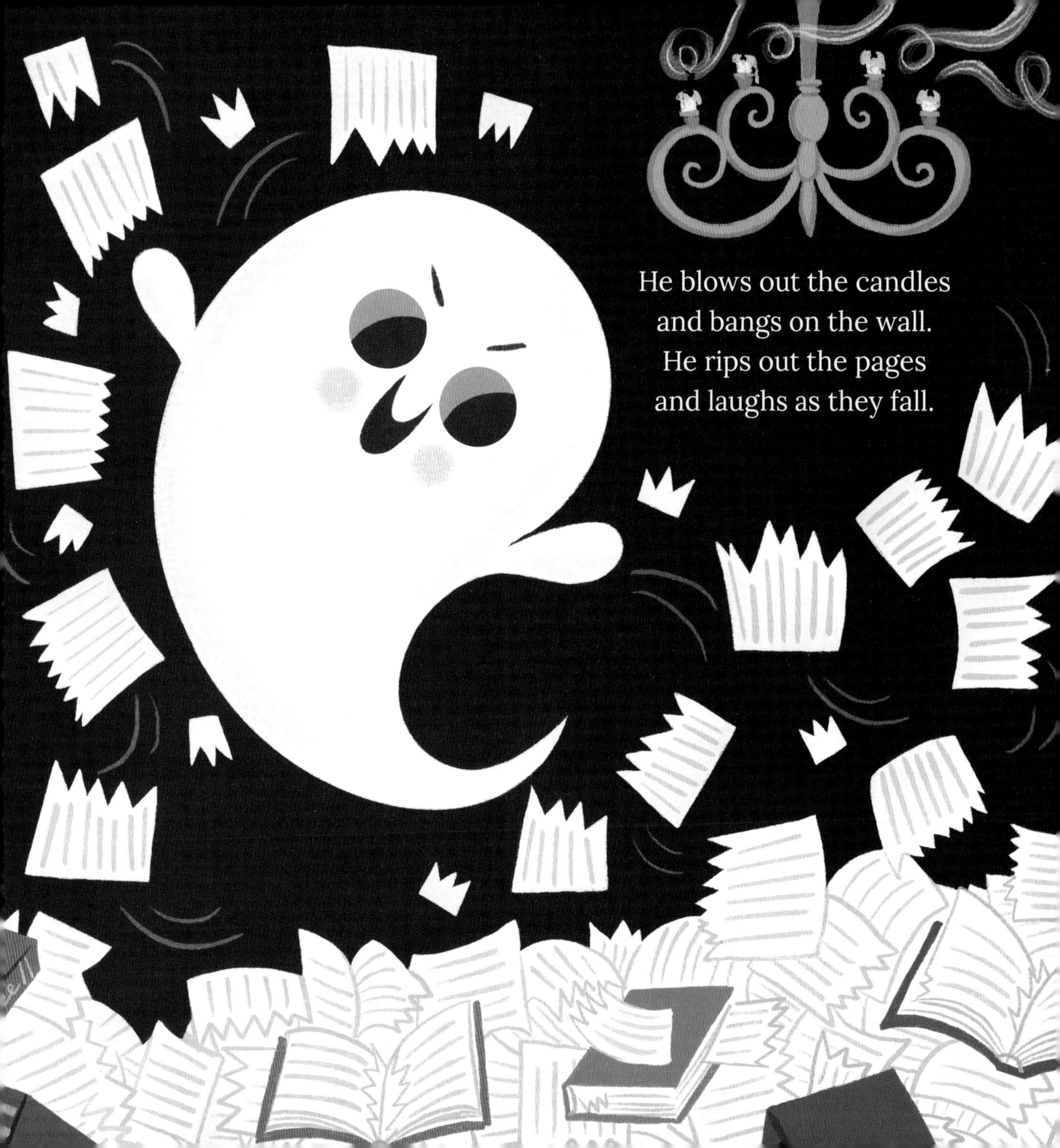

He blows out the candles
and bangs on the wall.
He rips out the pages
and laughs as they fall.

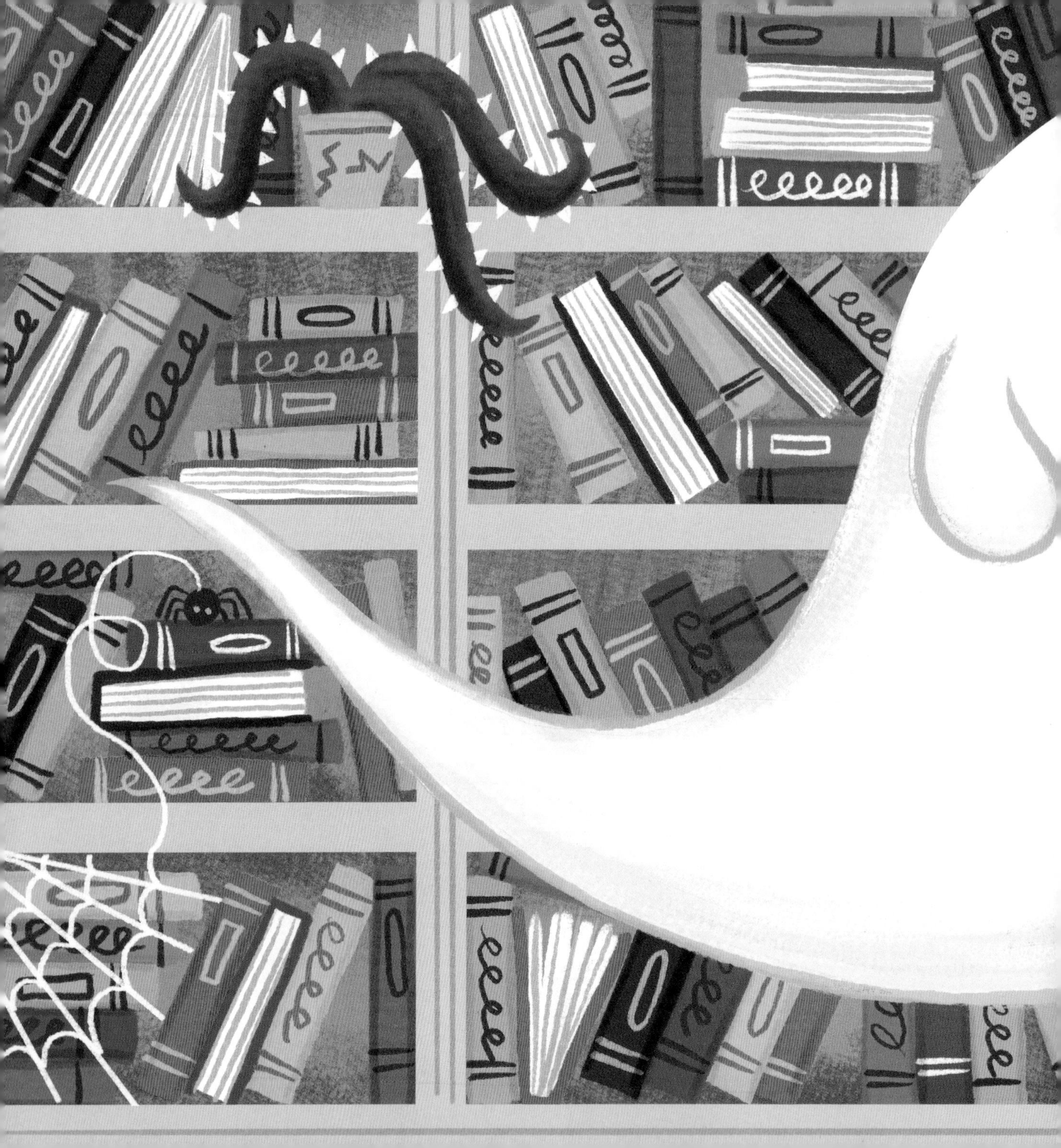

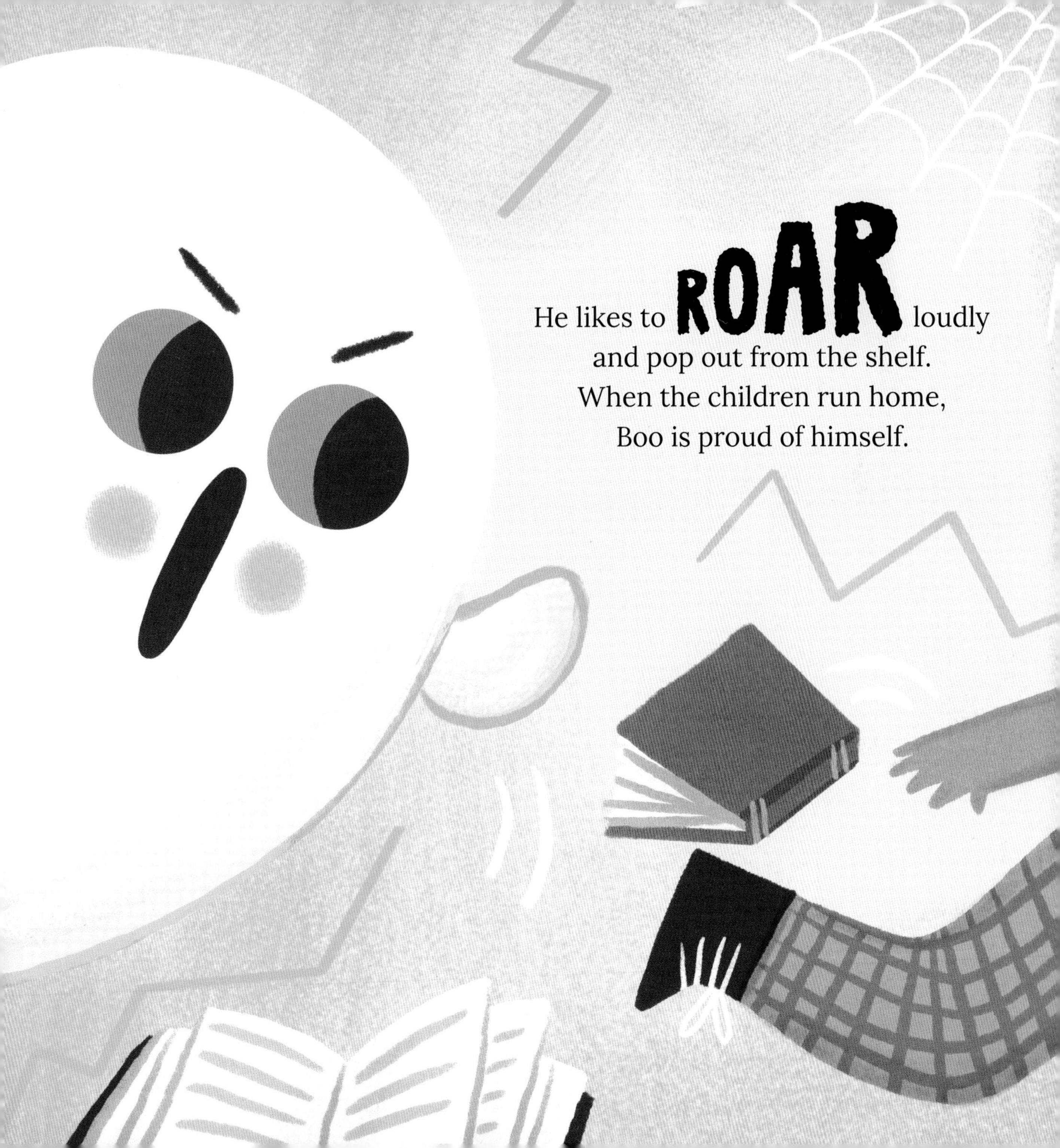

He likes to **ROAR** loudly
and pop out from the shelf.
When the children run home,
Boo is proud of himself.

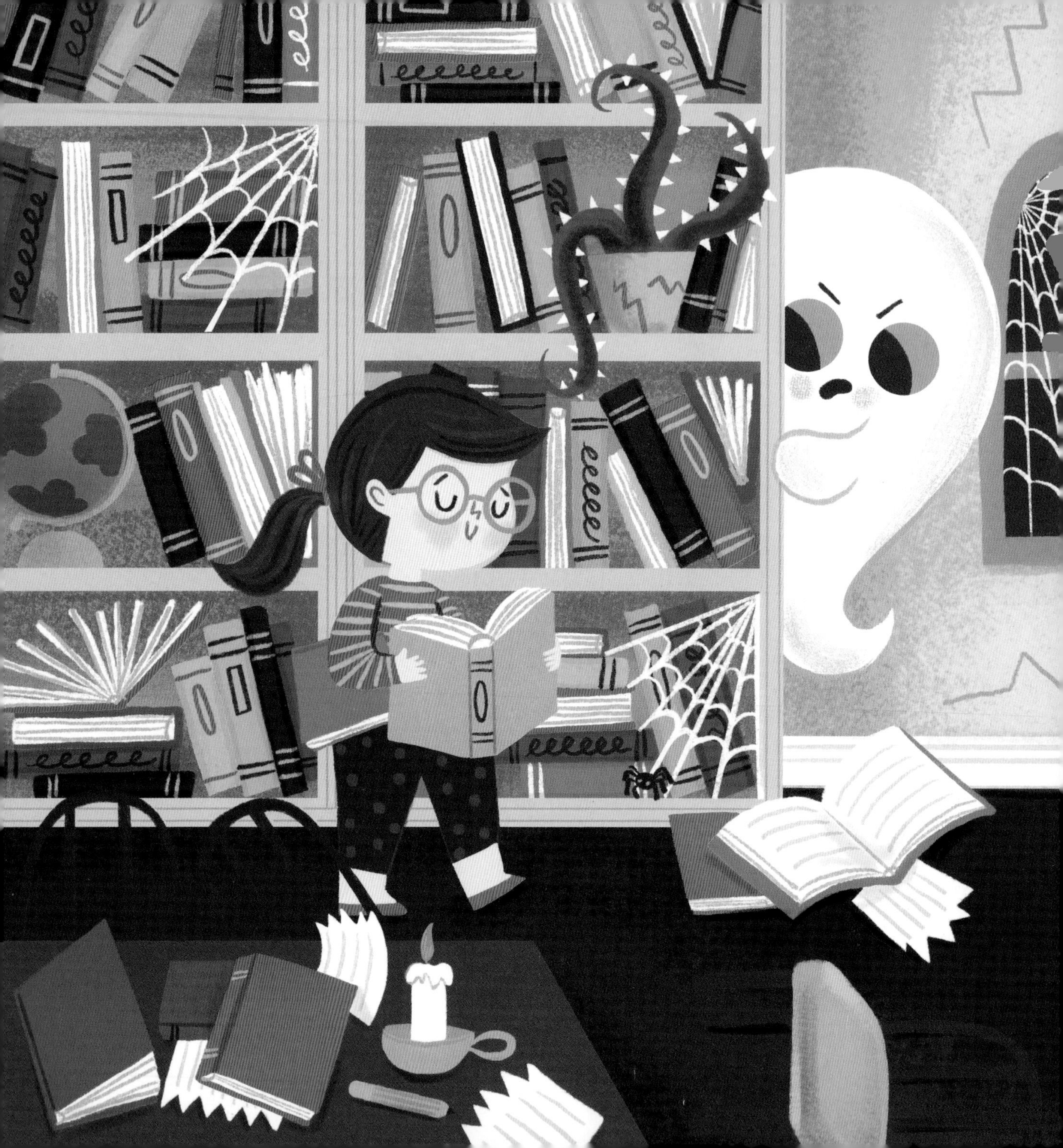

However, one Tuesday, one girl wasn't scared.
"This book is too good to put down," she declared.

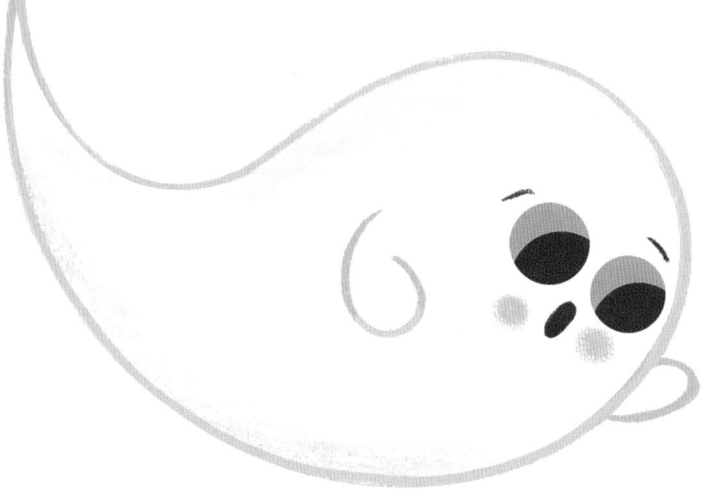

"My name is Poppy
and this chapter is so great.

Can you please be quiet,
so I can concentrate?"

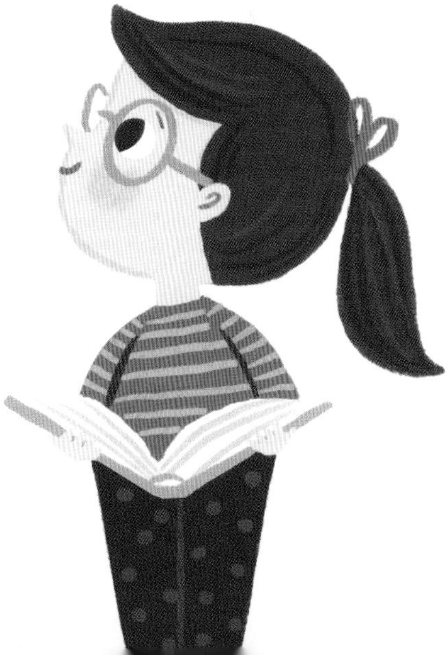

Boo shouted and howled, and he made his eyes **GLOW**.
He pushed over chairs, but Poppy still wouldn't go.

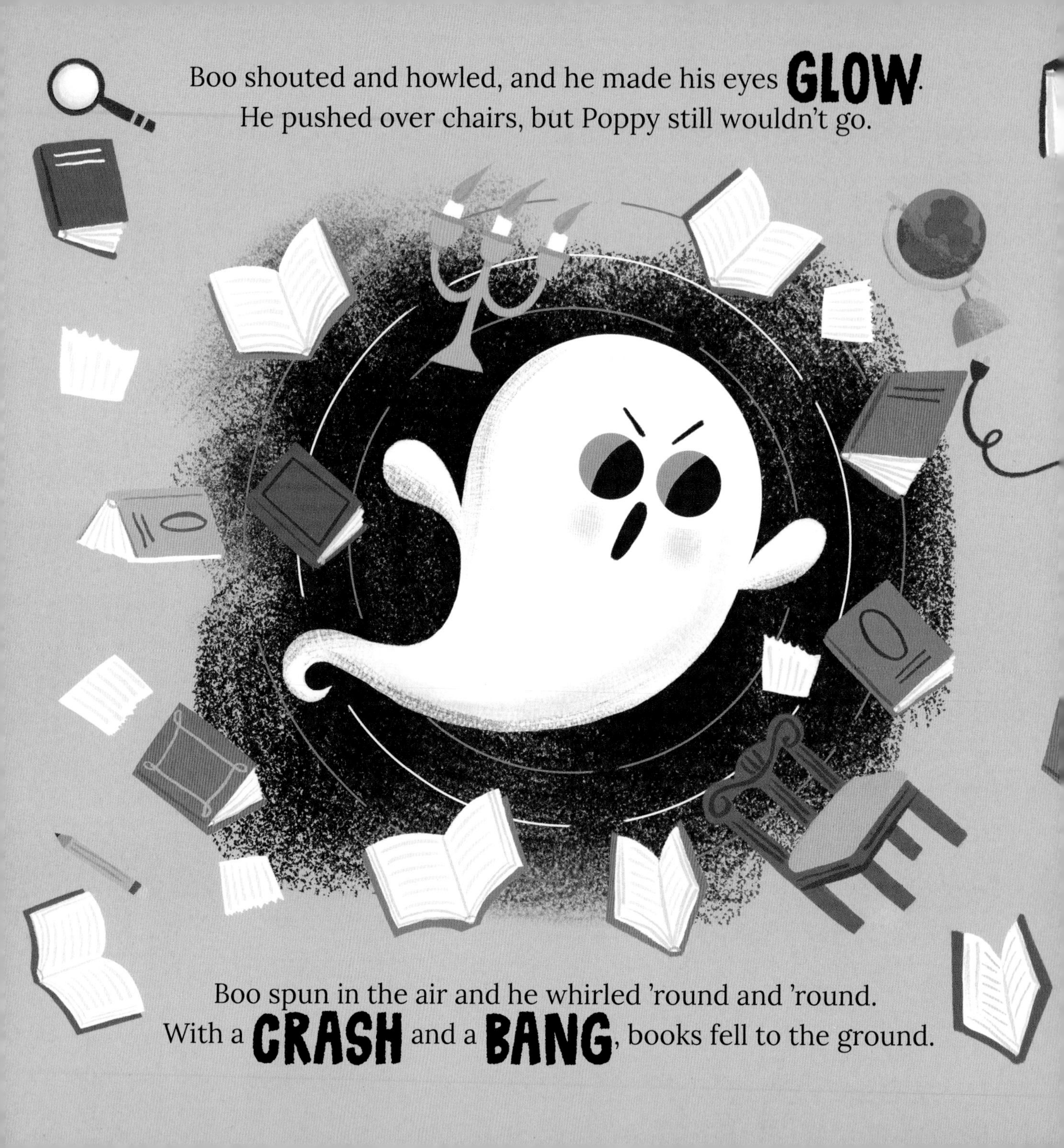

Boo spun in the air and he whirled 'round and 'round.
With a **CRASH** and a **BANG**, books fell to the ground.

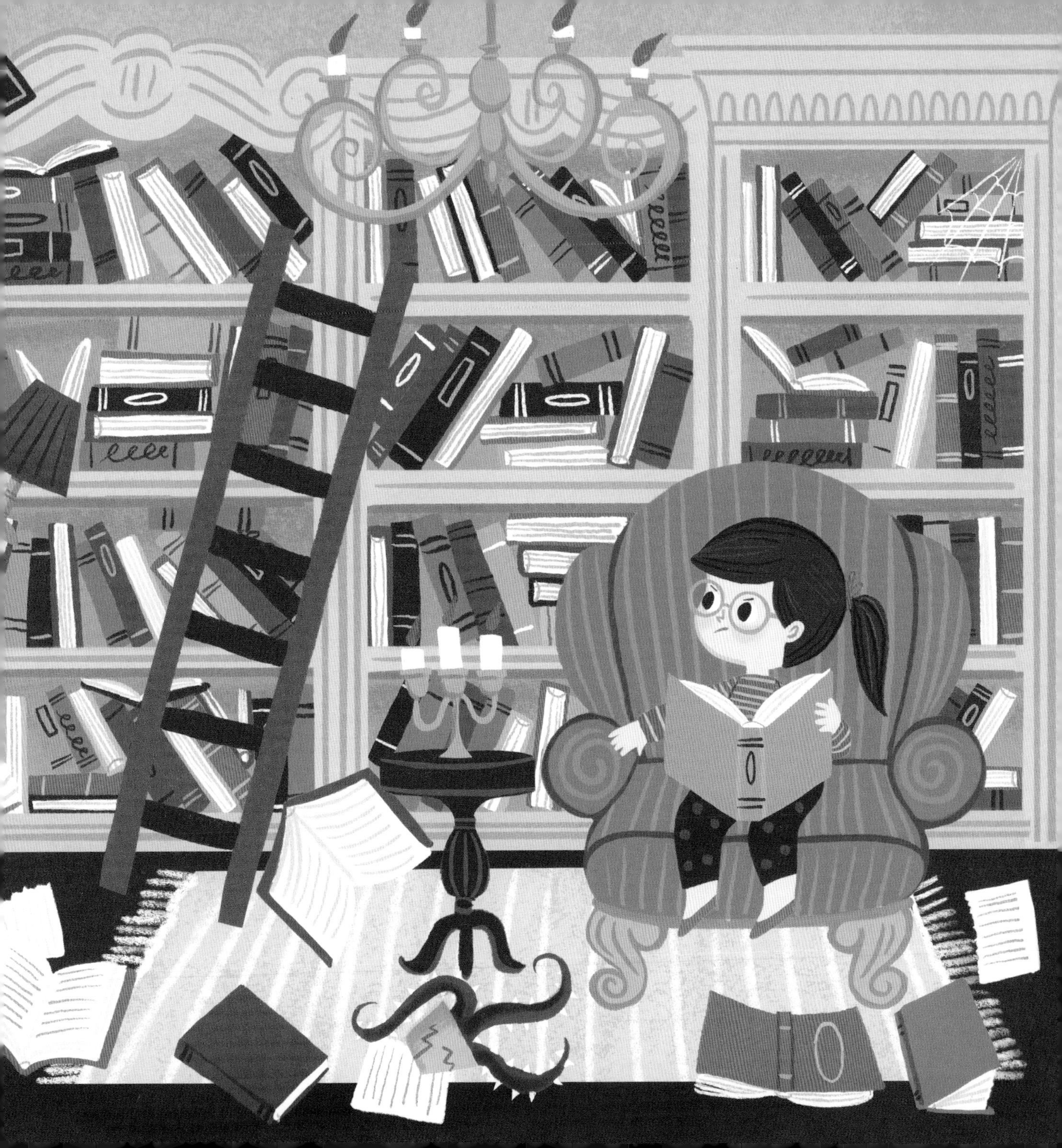

“Oh no, please don’t do that—what a big mess!
Readers would never do that to books . . . unless . . .”

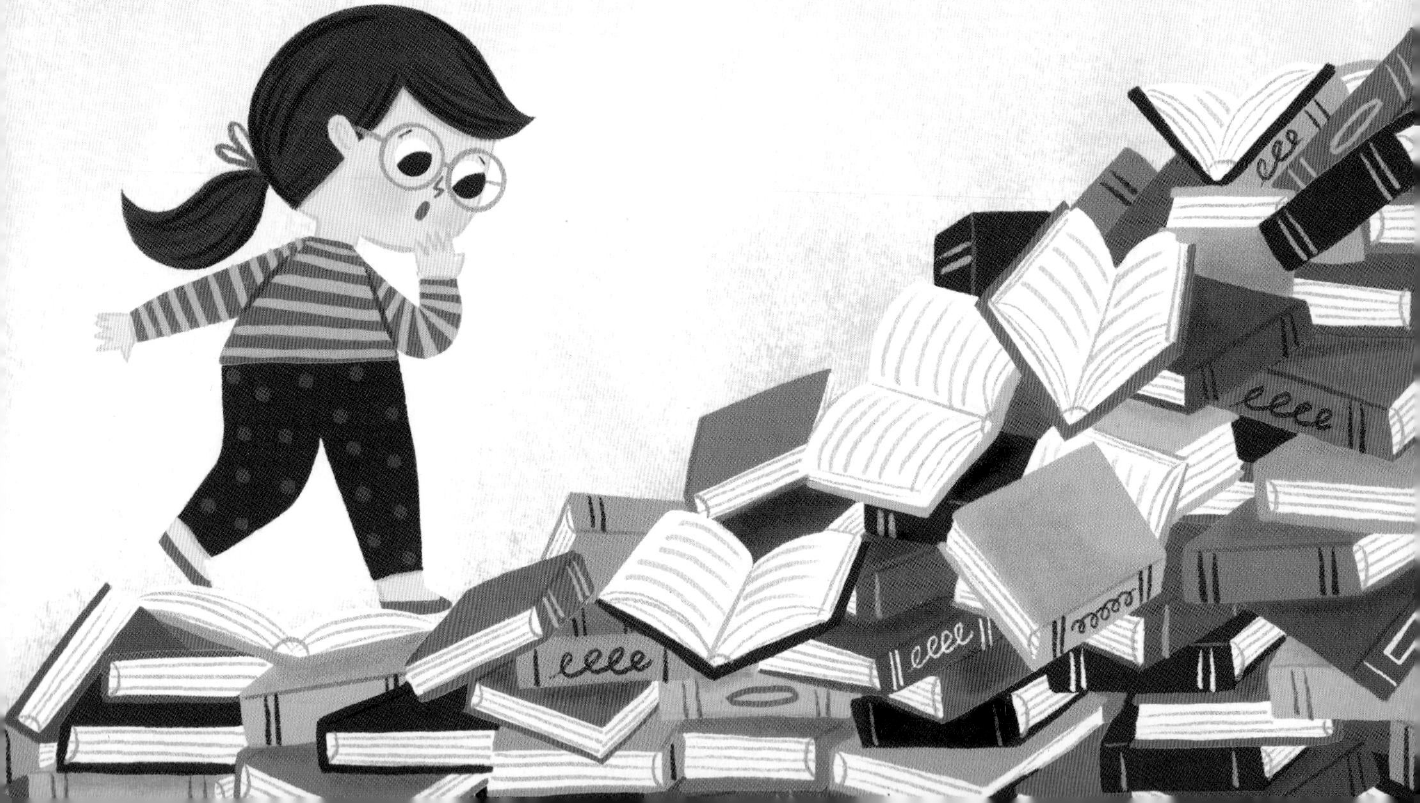

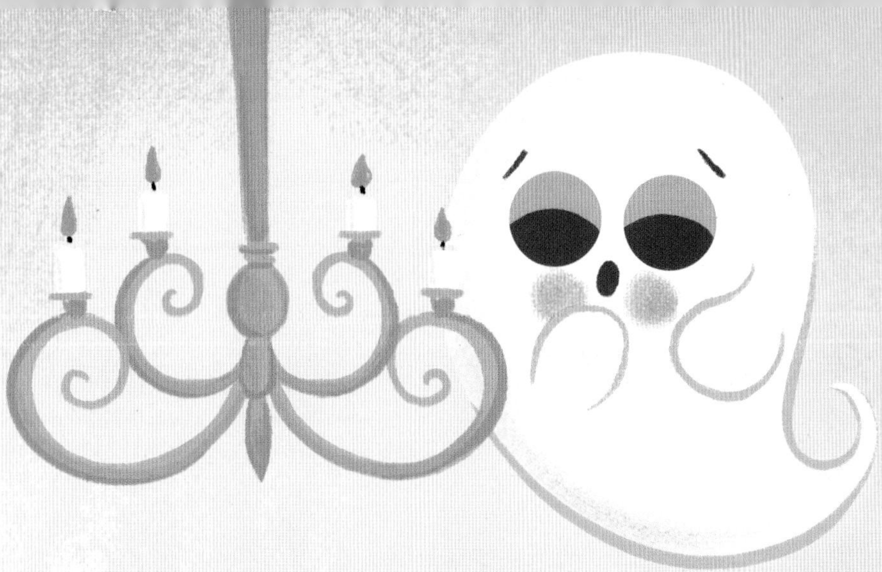

Boo's cheeks **BLUSHED** so brightly and that's when she knew,
Boo couldn't read yet—Poppy knew just what to do!

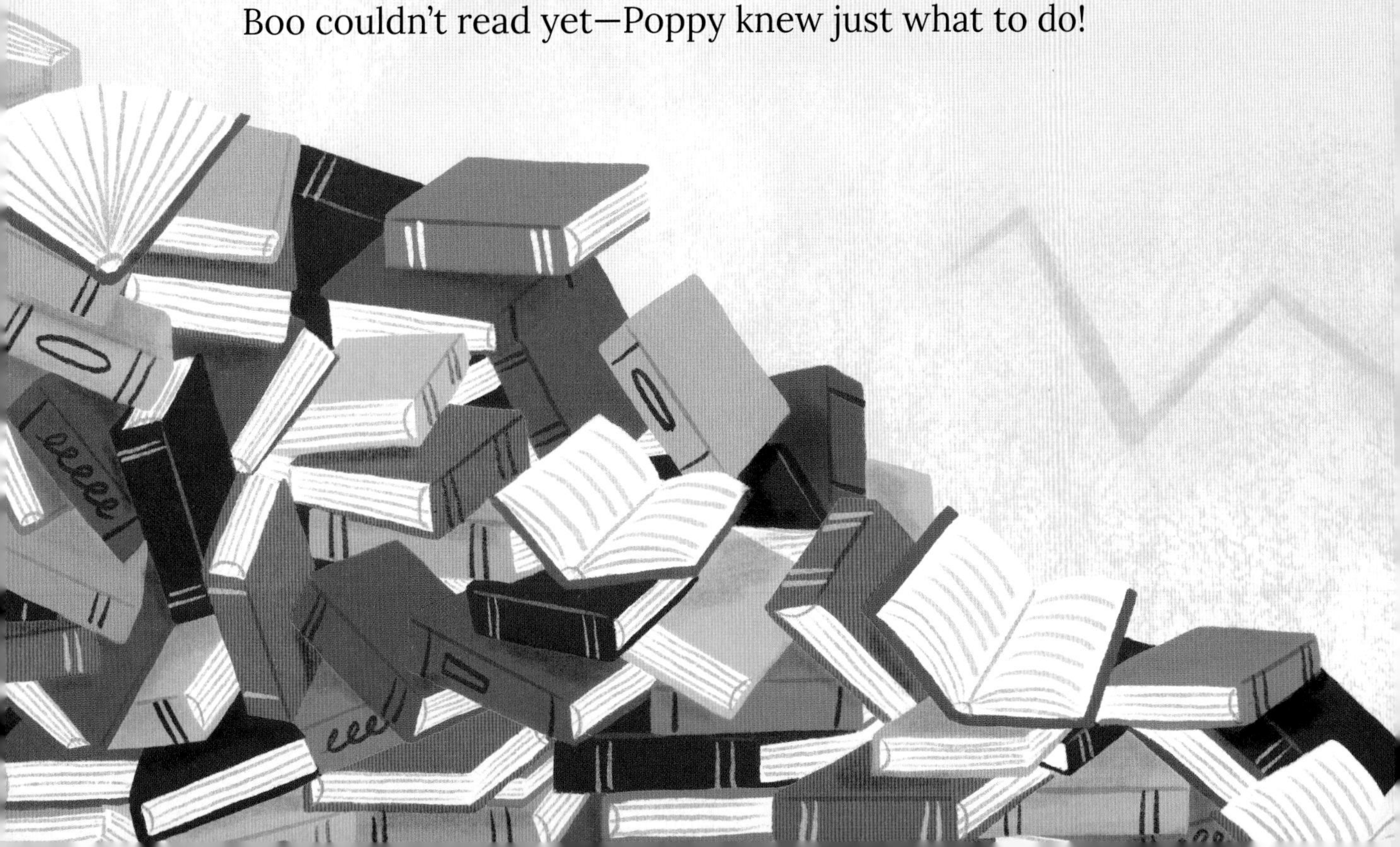

"Come sit down beside me, and I'll read to you.
Books are for everyone and that means you, too!"

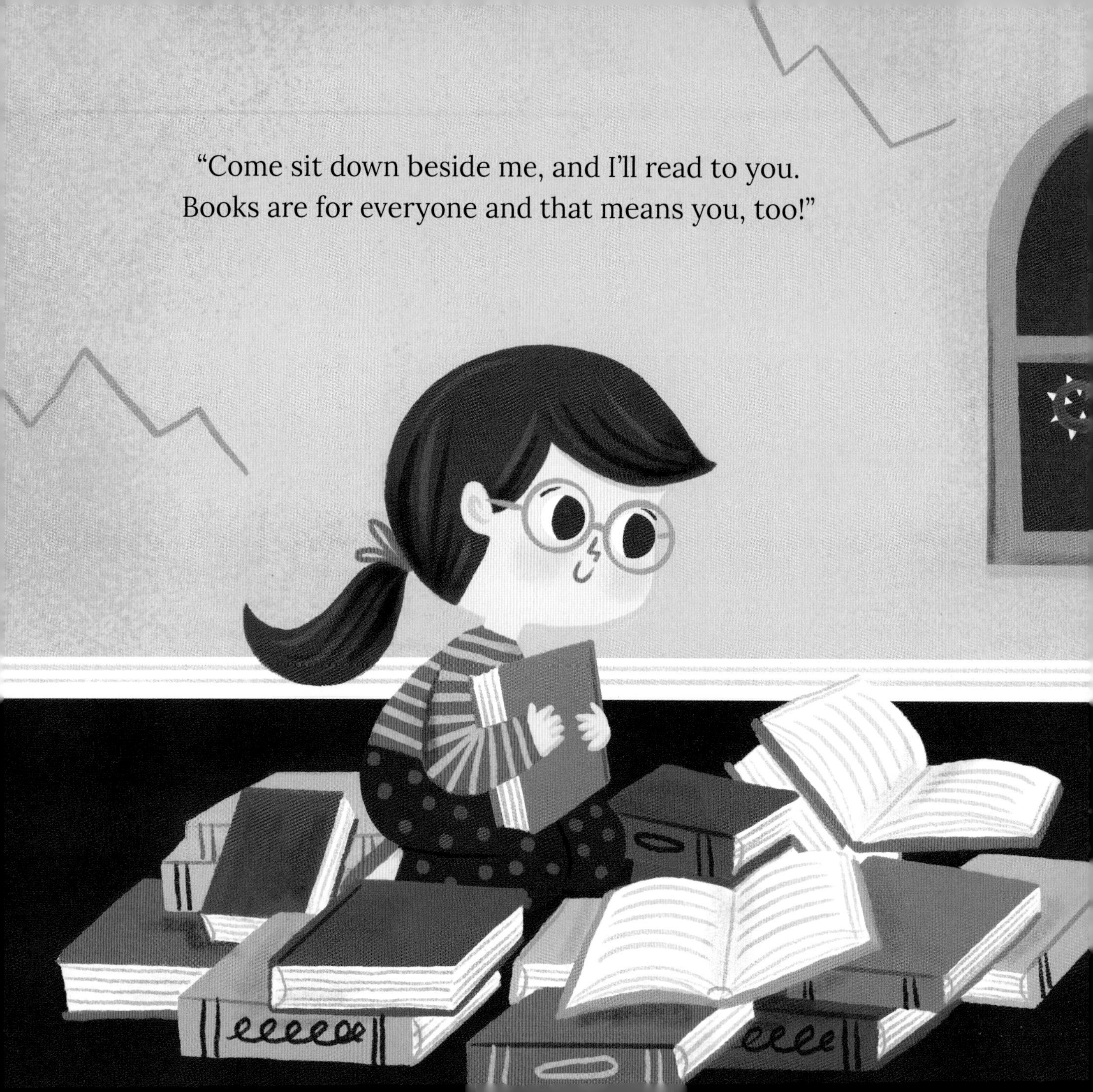

He wanted to join her, but he was **AFRAID**.
So instead he **GROWLED** loudly and kicked a lampshade.

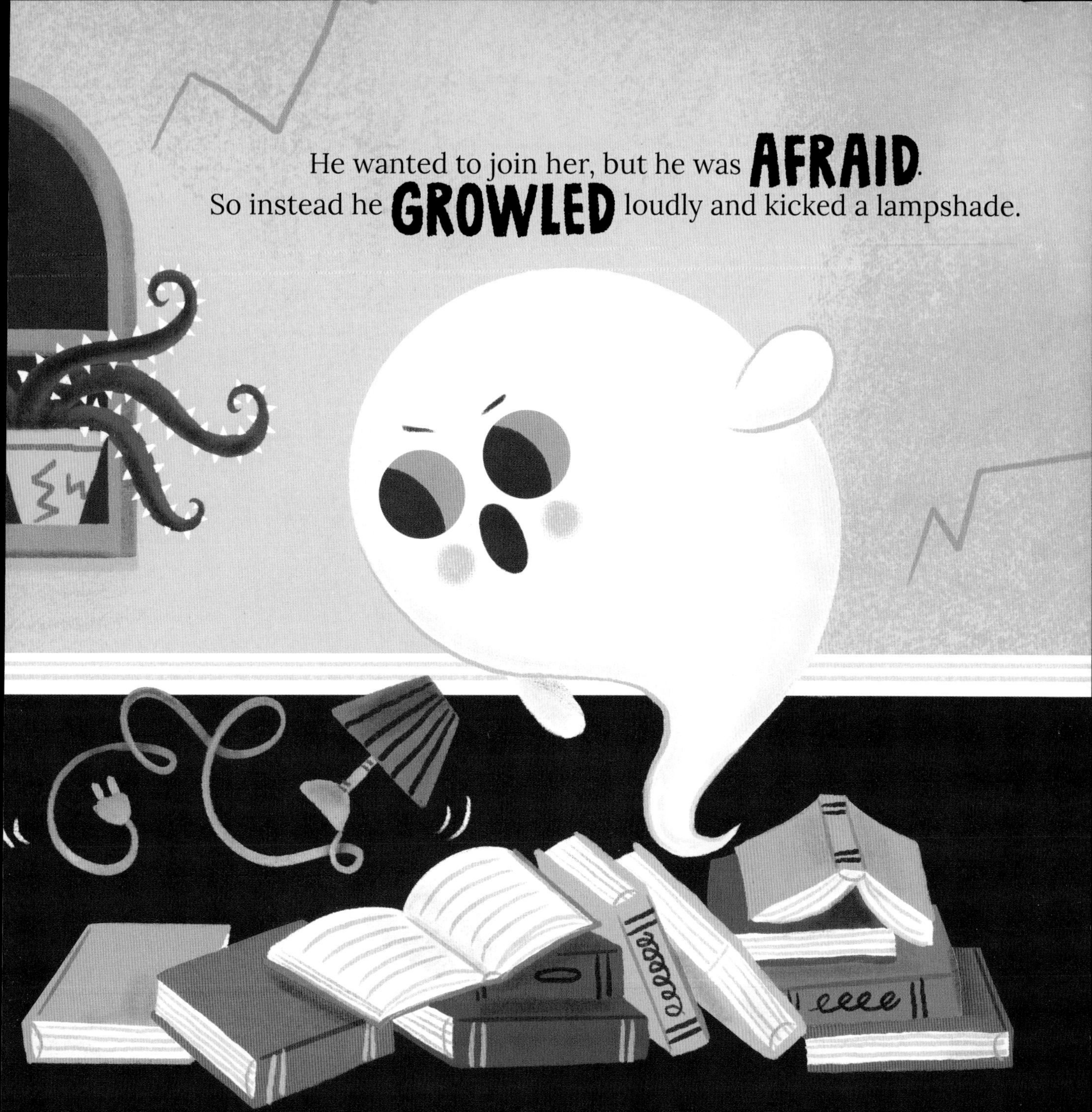

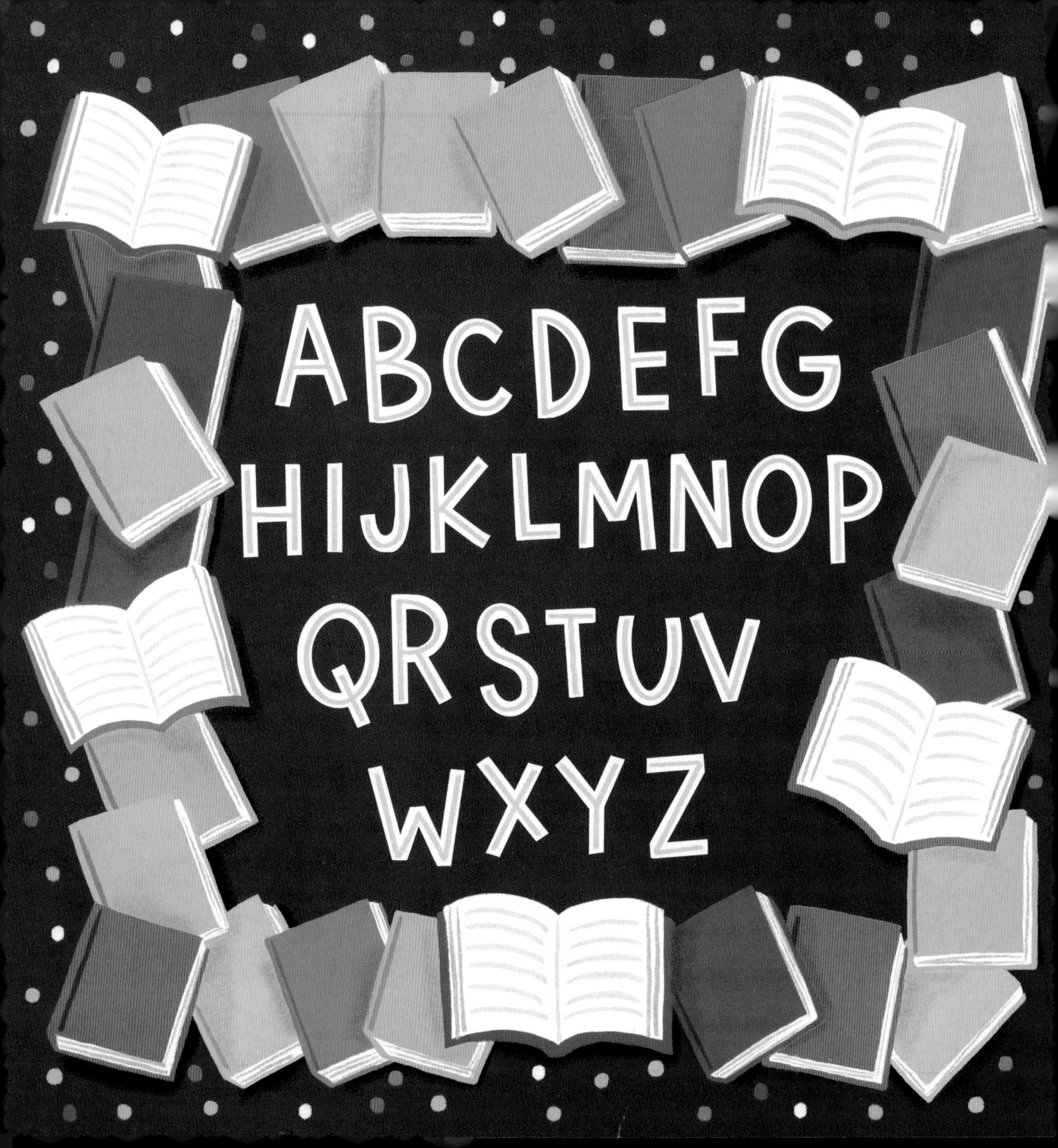
ABCDEFG
HIJKLMNOP
QRSTUV
WXYZ

"First, I'll teach you the letters, and then bit by bit,
you'll be reading words on your own! You can do it!"

Boo pouted and sat, but soon he agreed.
He spent hours with his new friend learning to read.

They read all kinds of books,
some short and some long.
There were so many choices,
they couldn't go wrong.

Poppy showed Boo fairy tales,
comic books, and some plays,
biographies and short stories—
they explored them for days!

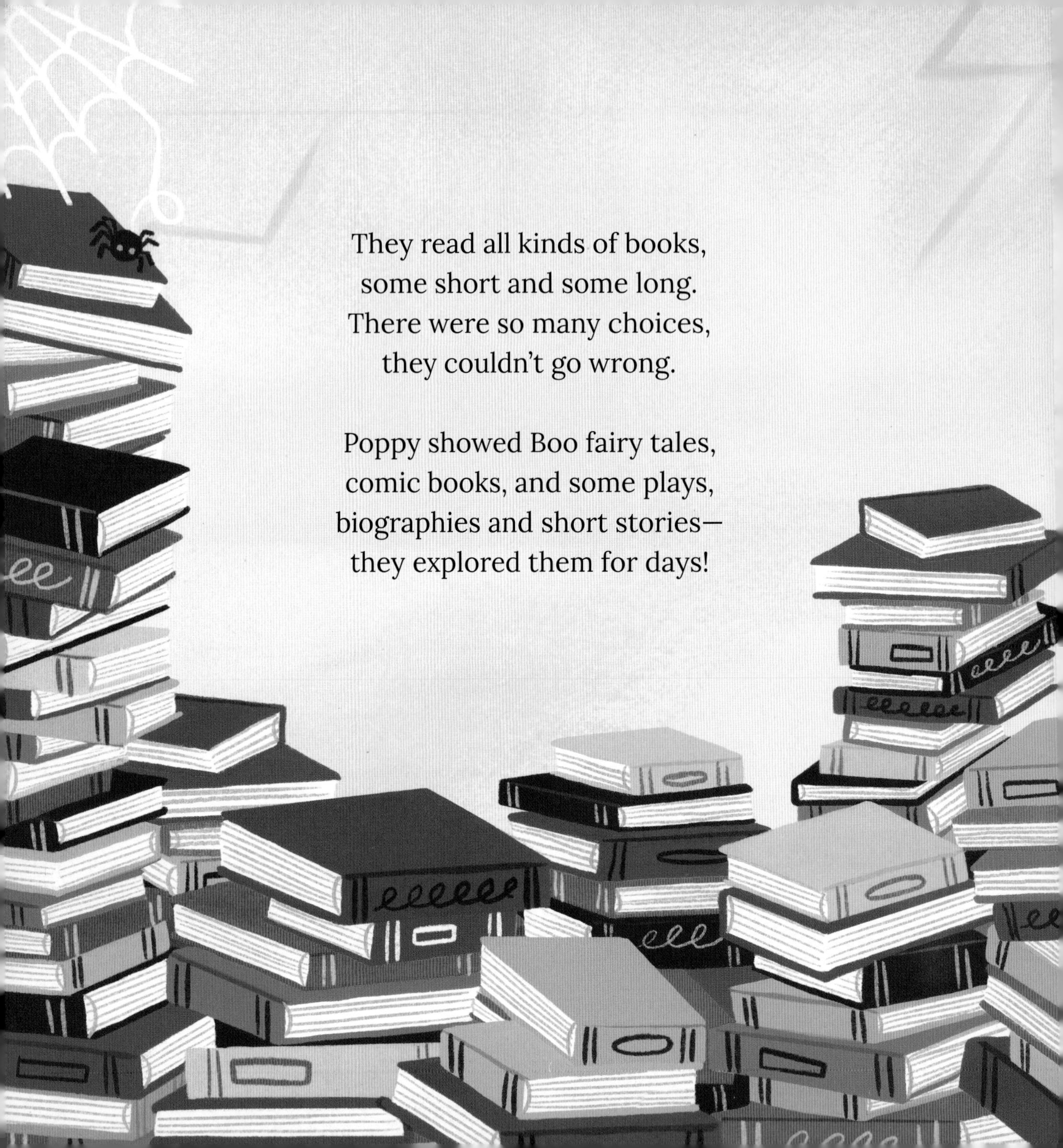

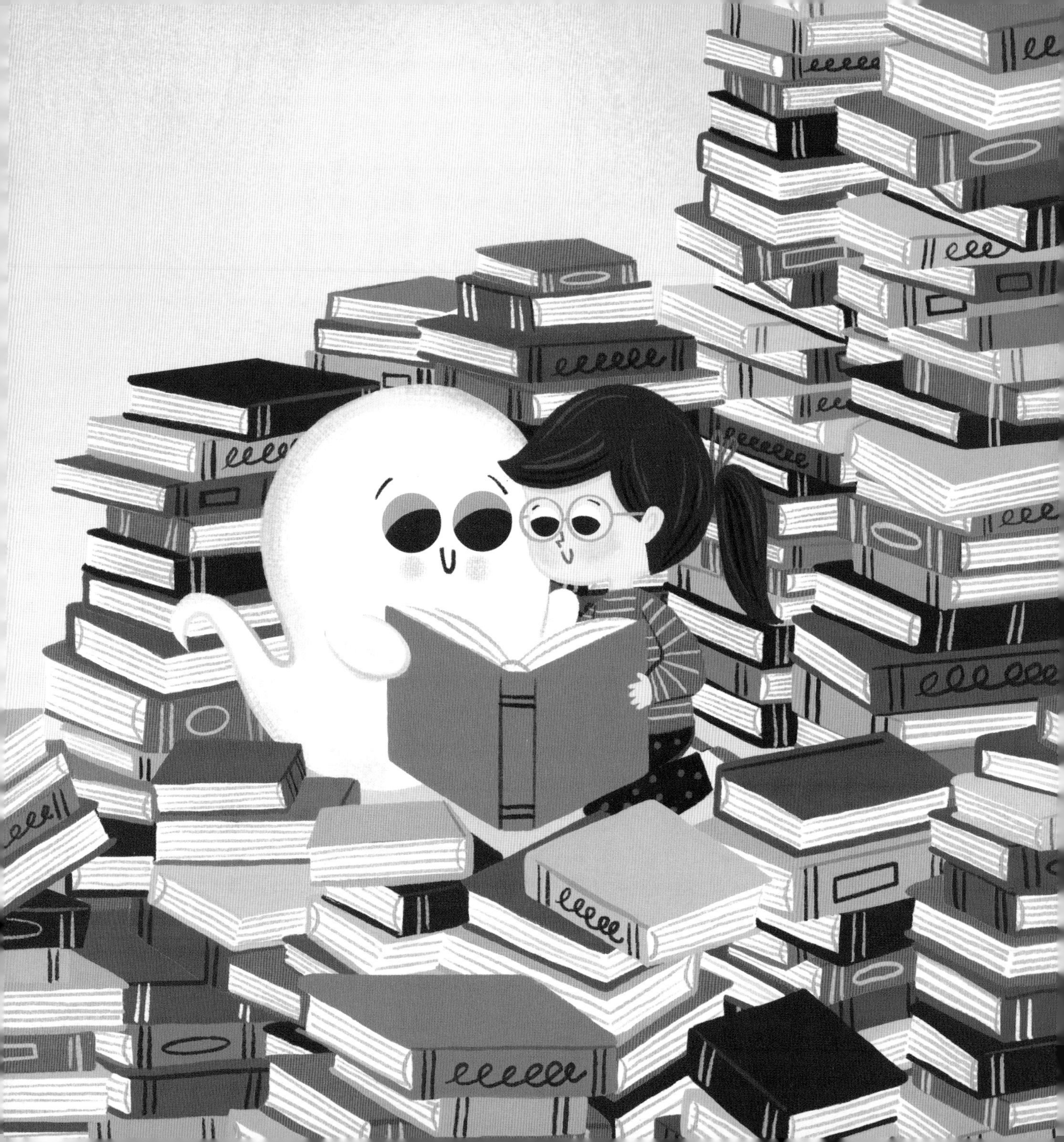

Boo added some mysteries
and poems to the pile.
His eyes became bright,
and he grew such a big smile!

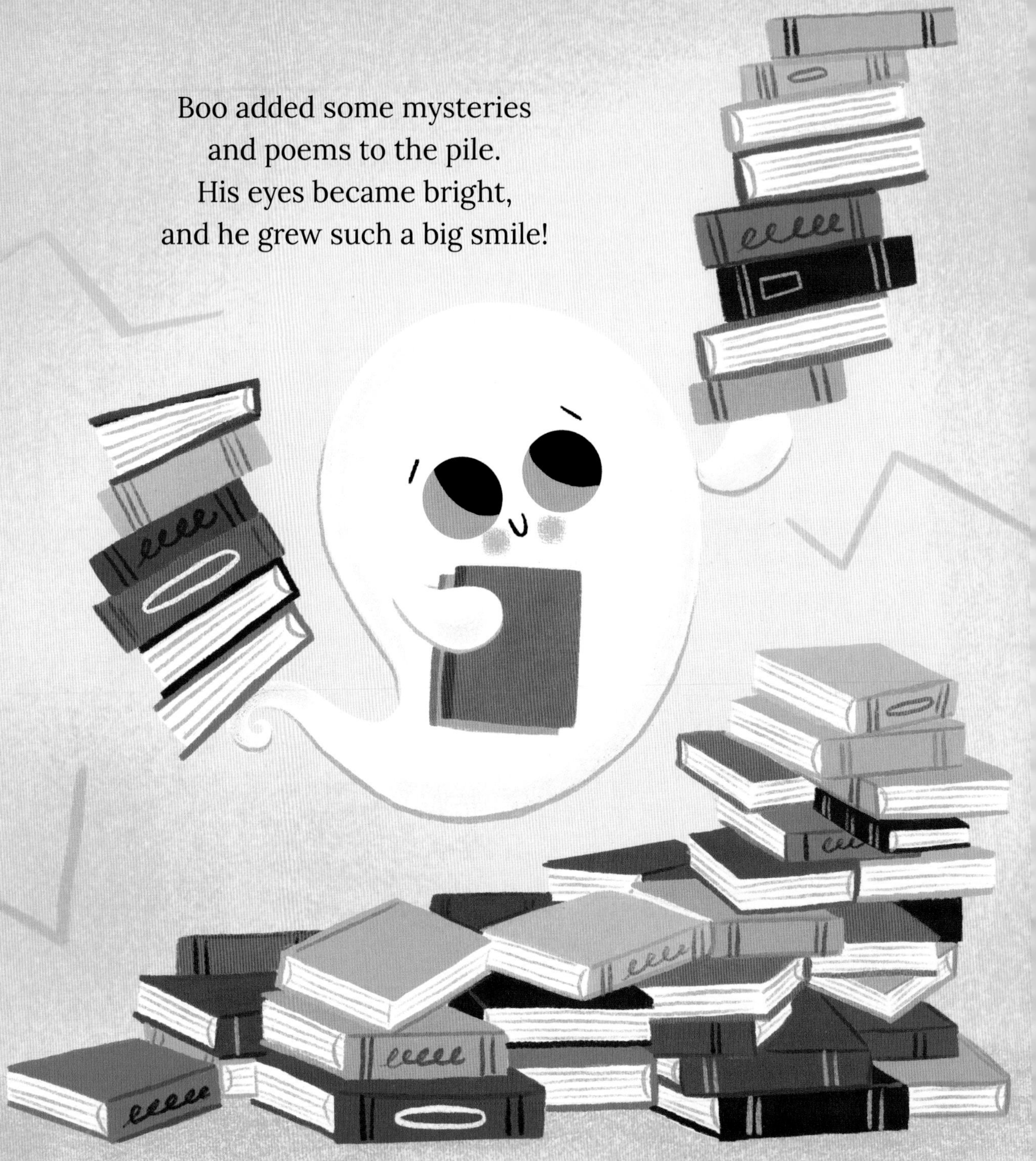

There was something about him
that wasn't the same.

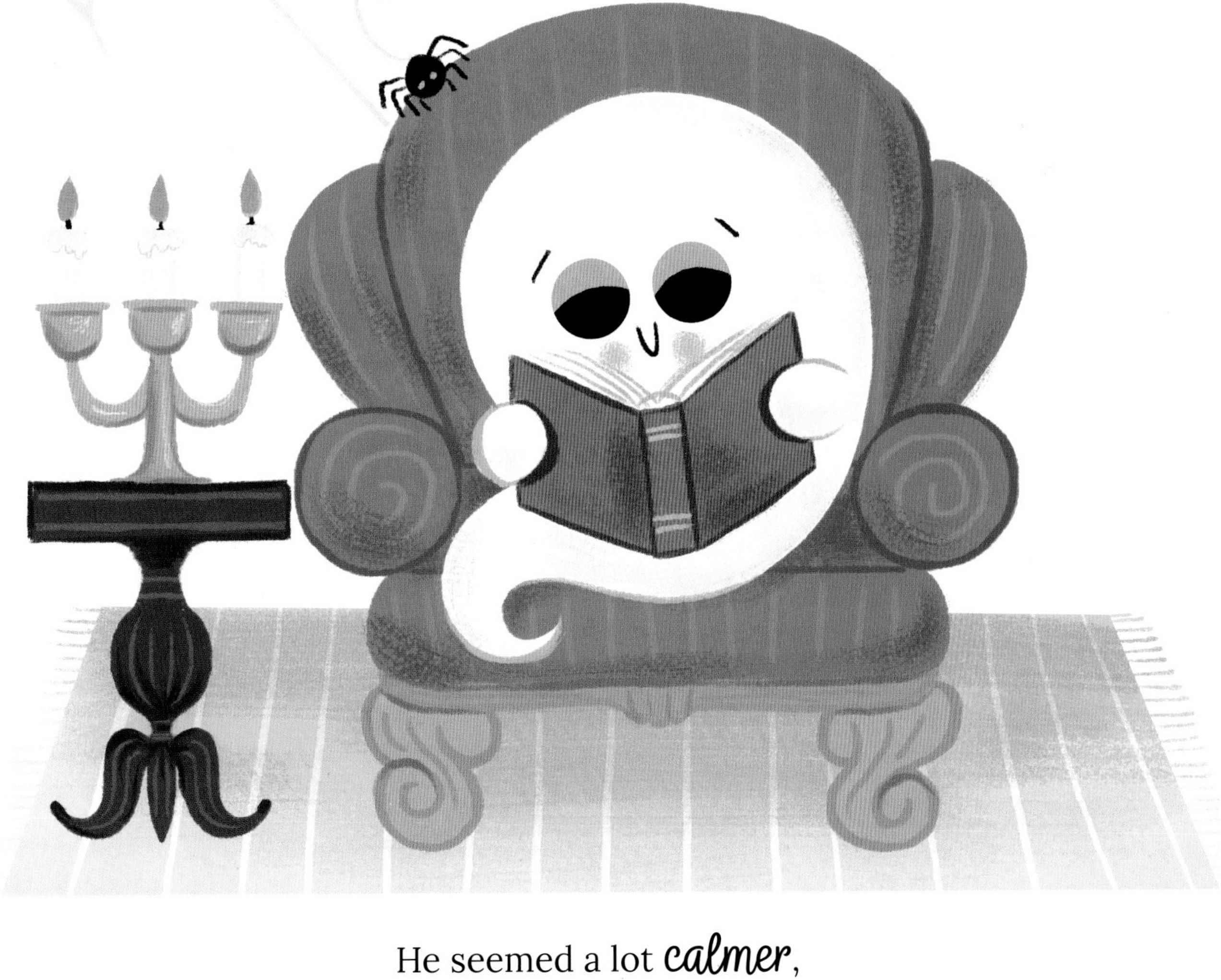

He seemed a lot *calmer*,
a little more *tame*.

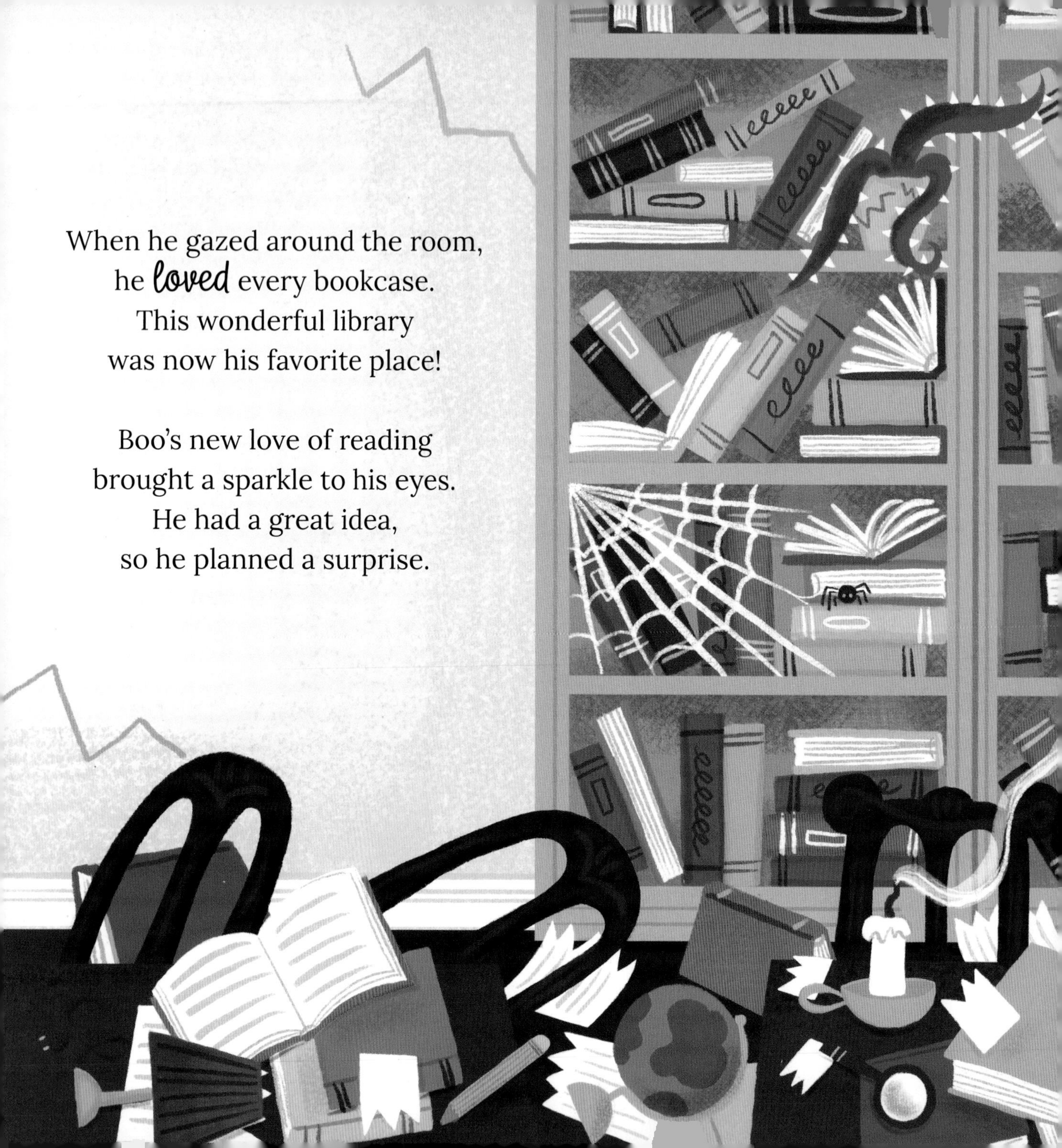

When he gazed around the room,
he *loved* every bookcase.
This wonderful library
was now his favorite place!

Boo's new love of reading
brought a sparkle to his eyes.
He had a great idea,
so he planned a surprise.

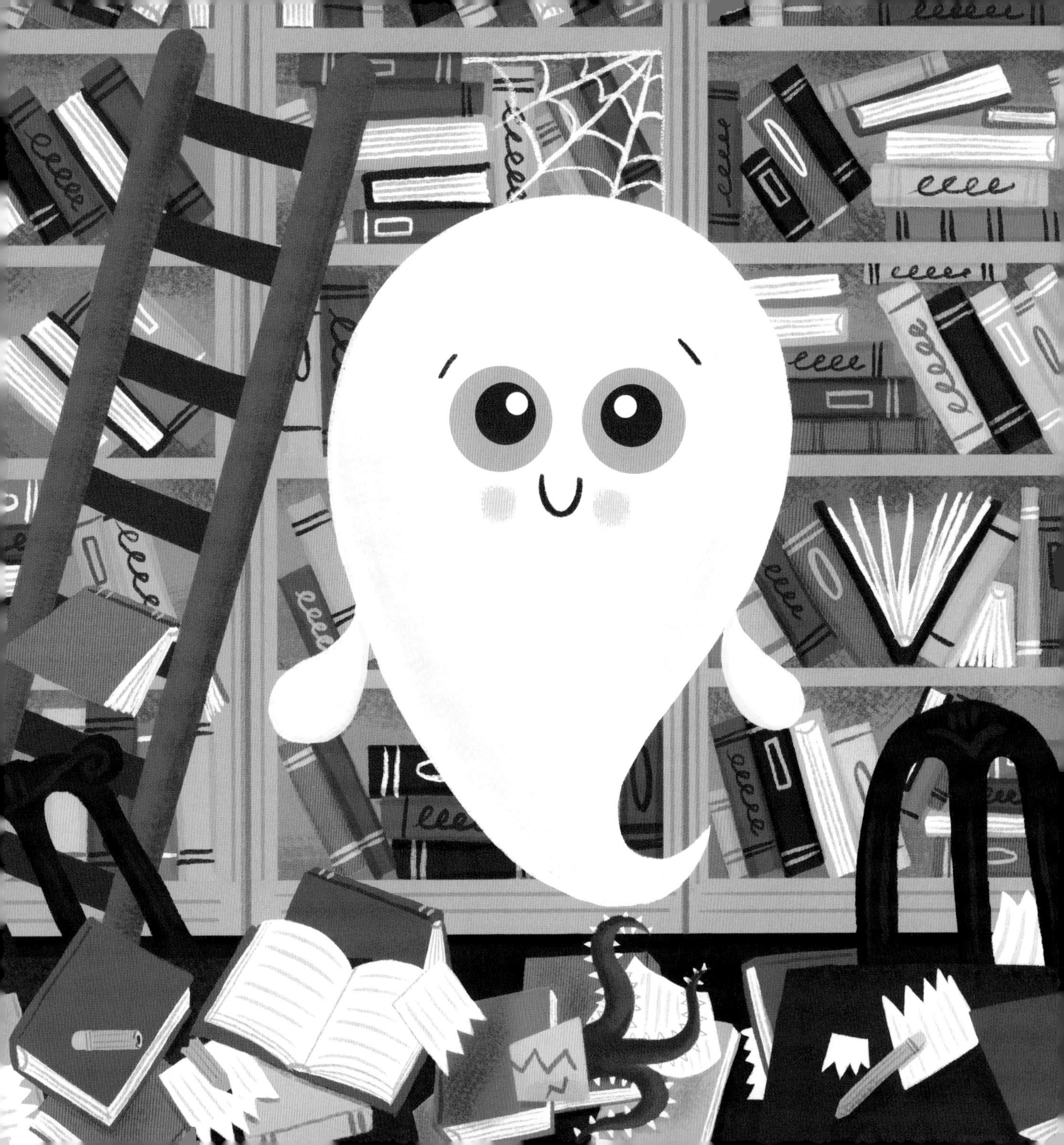

The following morning,
the library was changed.

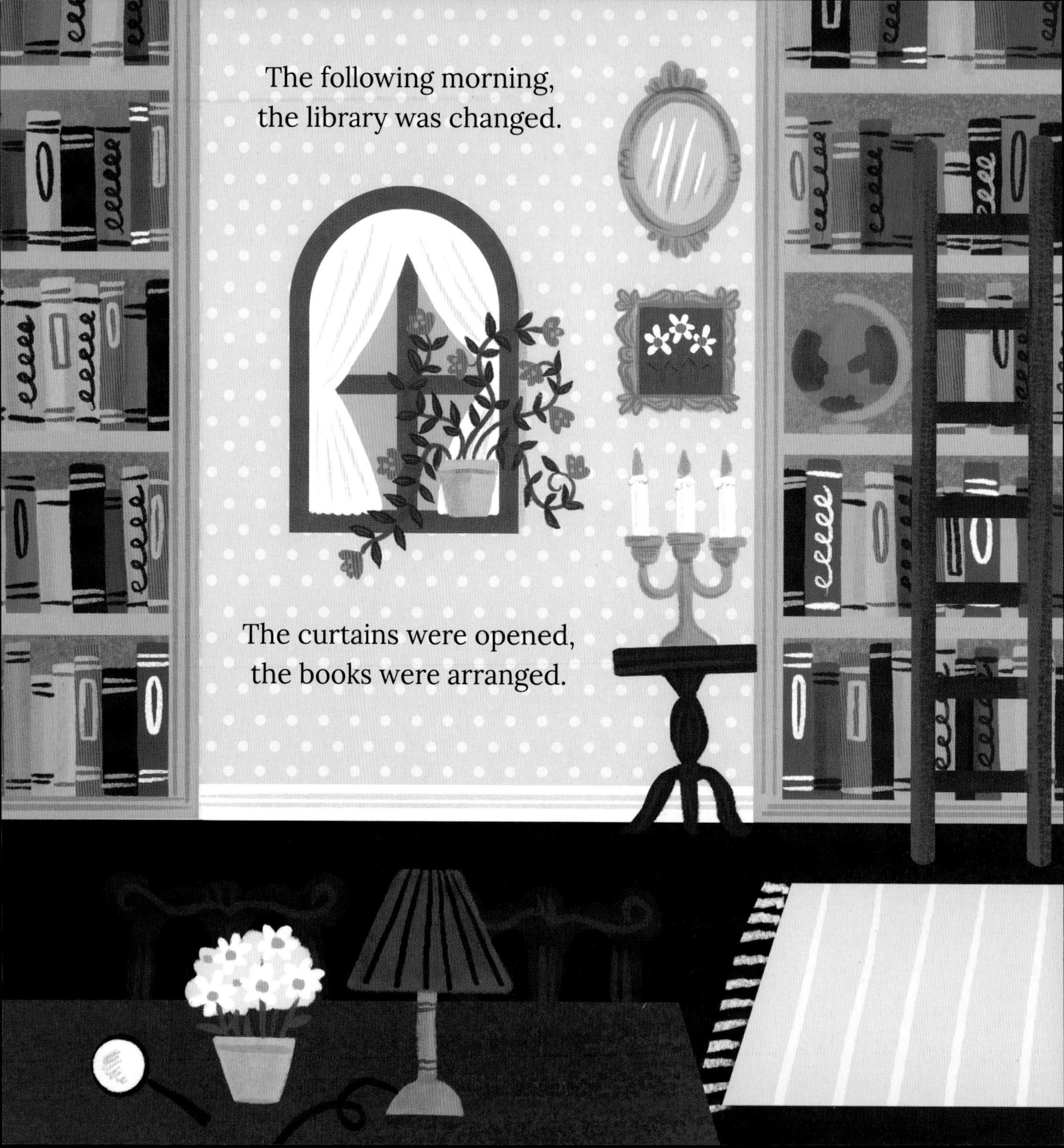

The curtains were opened,
the books were arranged.

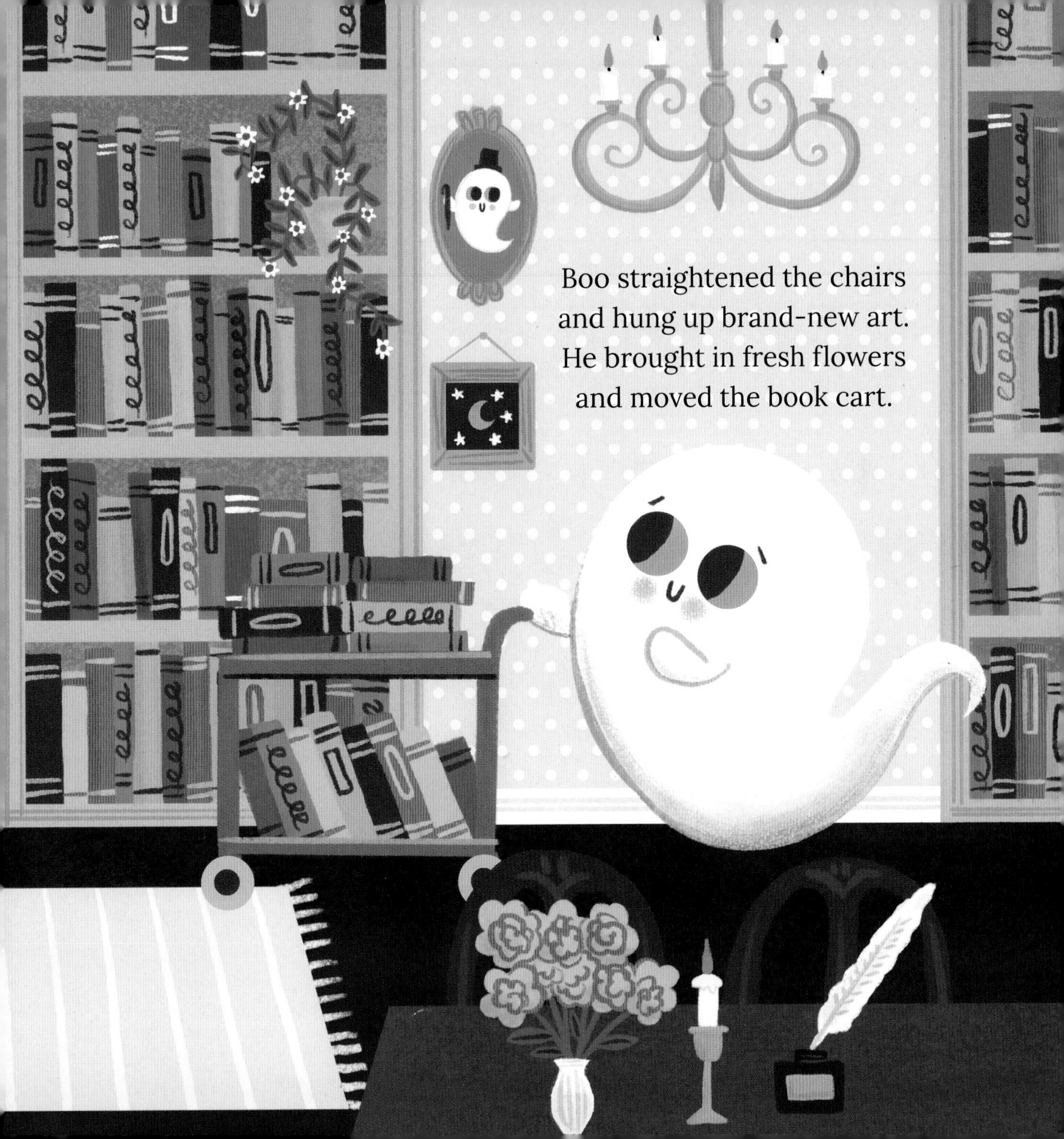

Boo straightened the chairs
and hung up brand-new art.
He brought in fresh flowers
and moved the book cart.

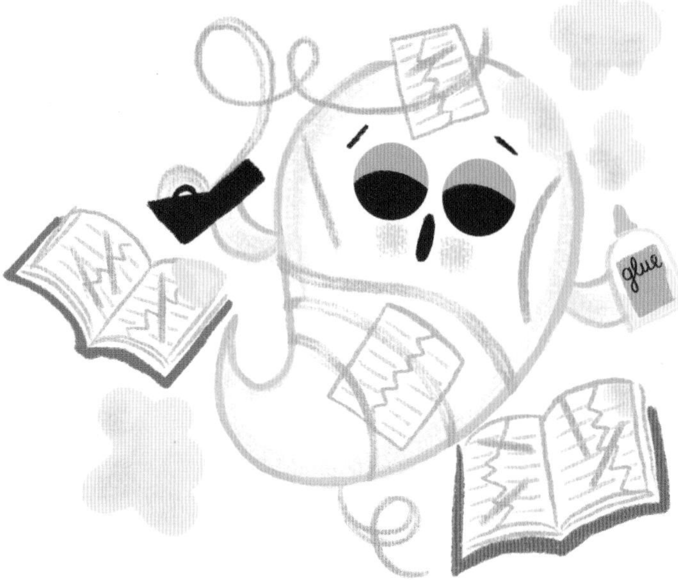
glue

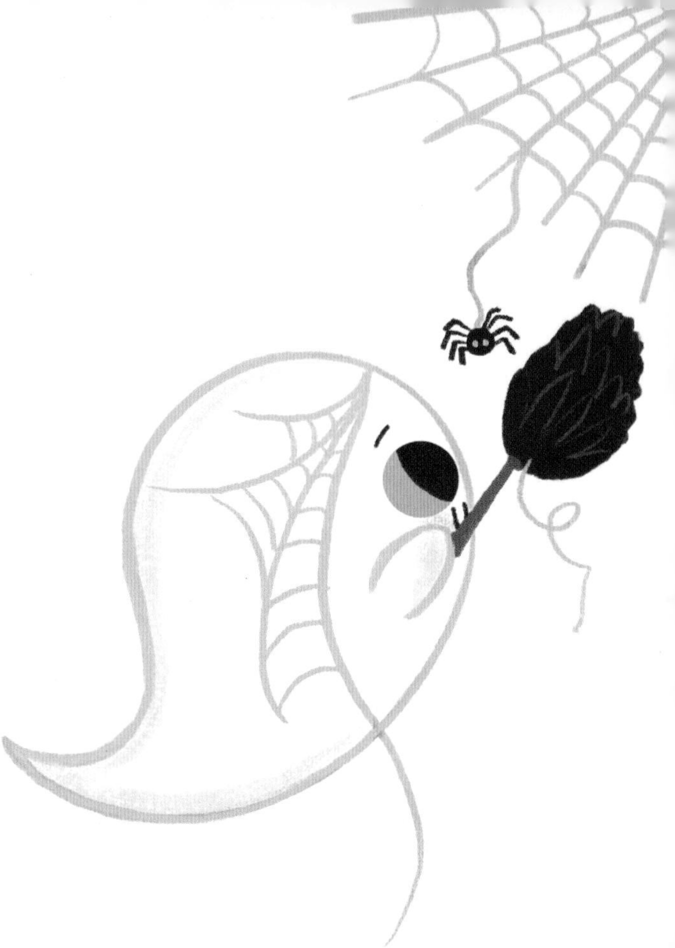

Boo fixed the ripped pages
and dusted up high,

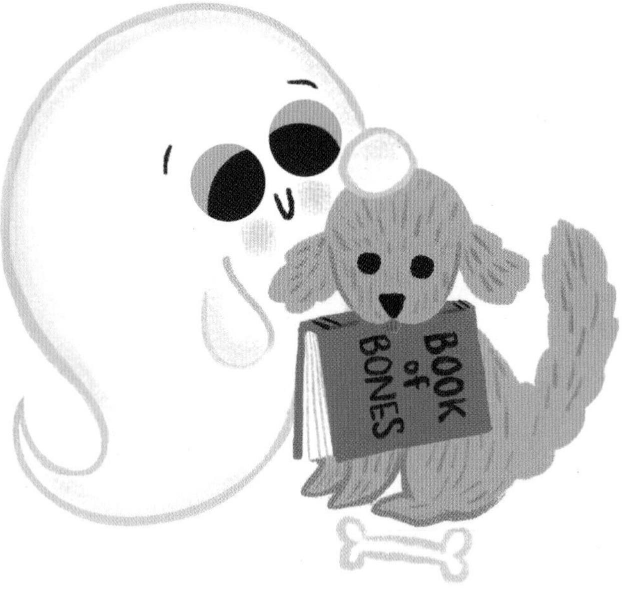
BOOK
of
BONES

and happily helped
all the guests that came by.

Boo helped select picture books as kids sat and read.
He helped them with big words—
"Thank you, Boo!" they all said.

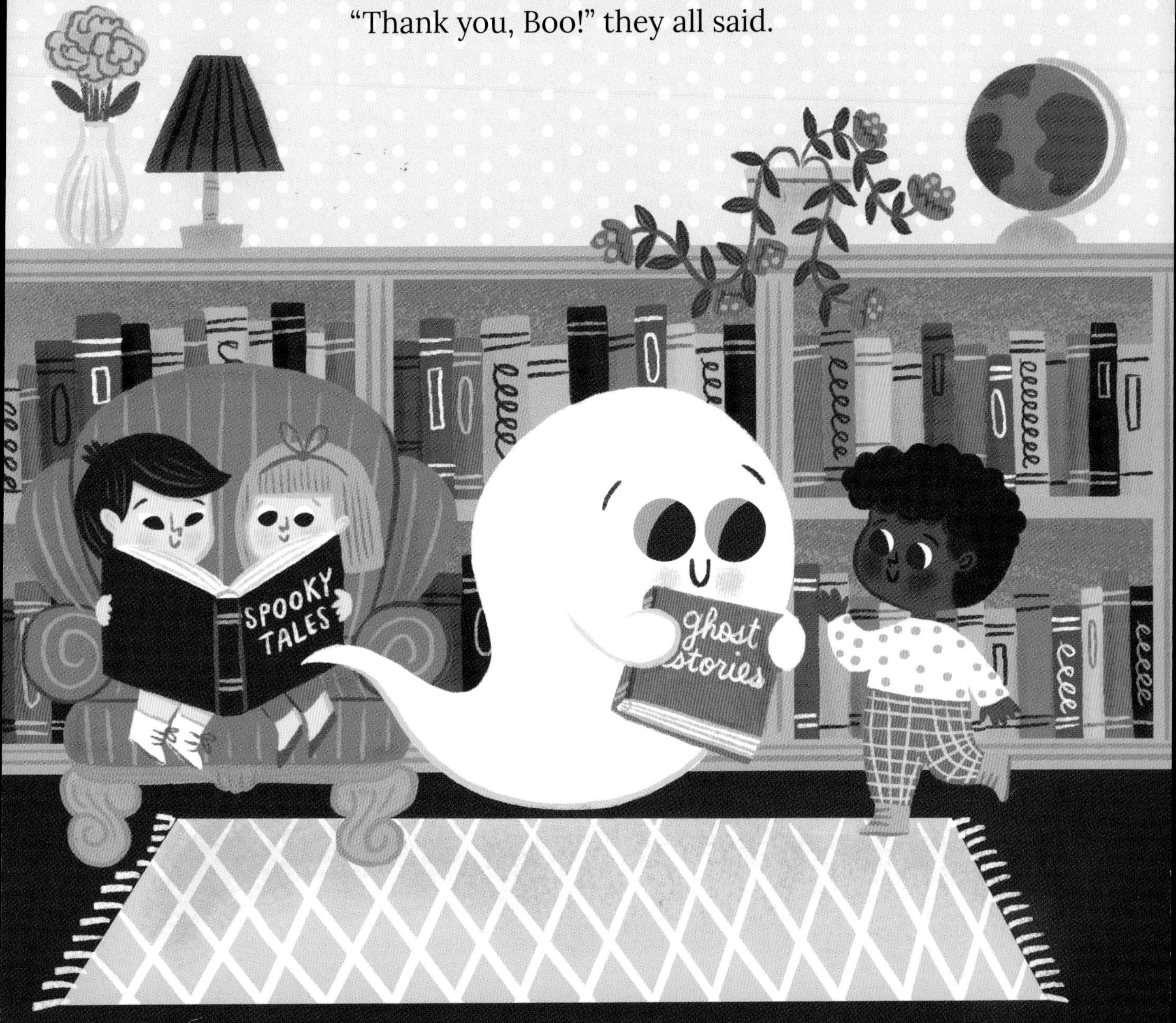
SPOOKY TALES
ghost stories

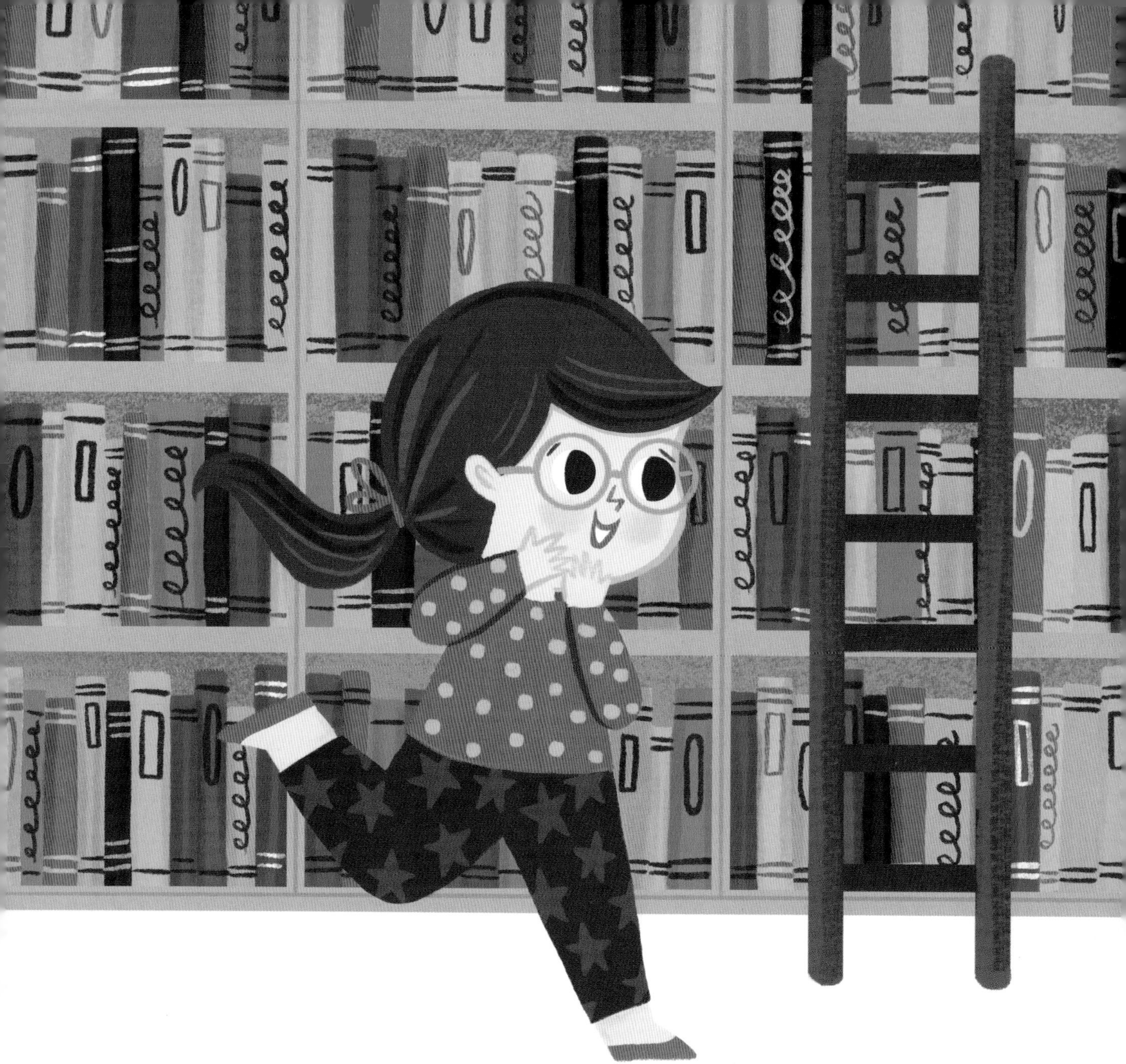

Later that evening, Poppy came in for a book.
She was thrilled and surprised with the library's new look.

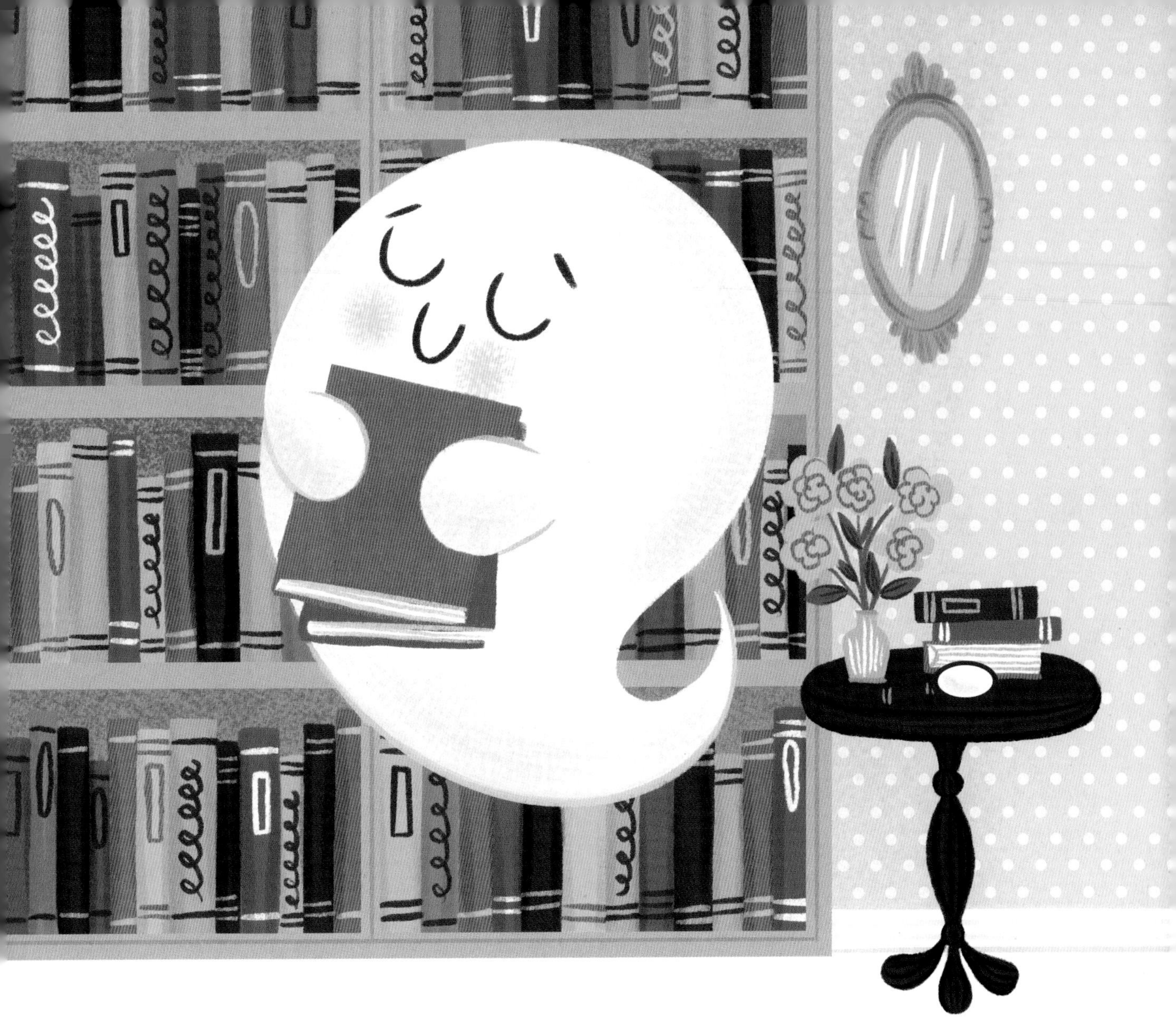

Poppy greeted her friend Boo and examined his face.
He was beaming with *pride* at what he'd done with the space.

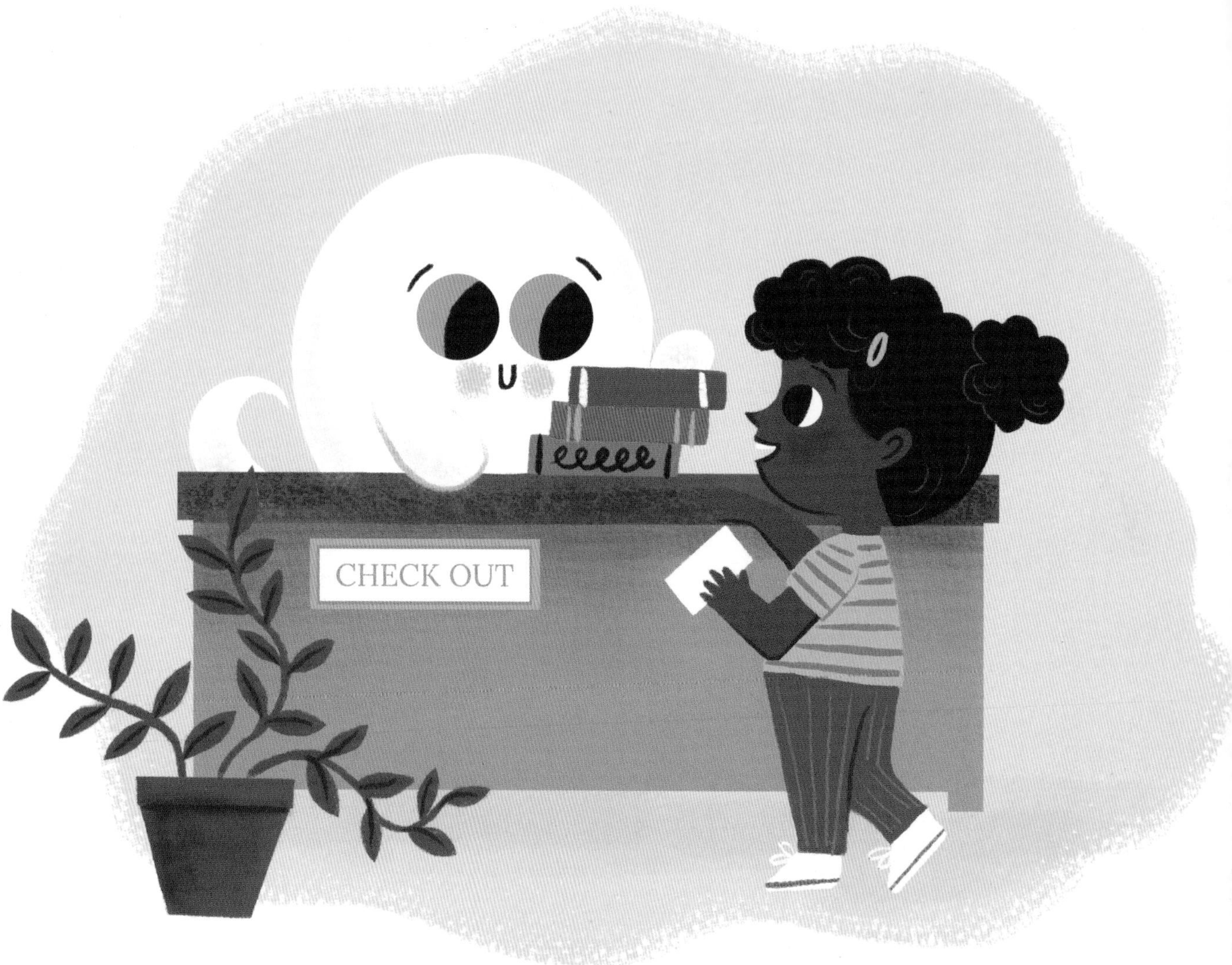
CHECK OUT

After checking out books,
he'd get his own reading done.
It had been so many years since
he'd had so much fun.

When the library doors closed,
he said, "Come back soon!"
And then he read poetry
by the light of the moon.

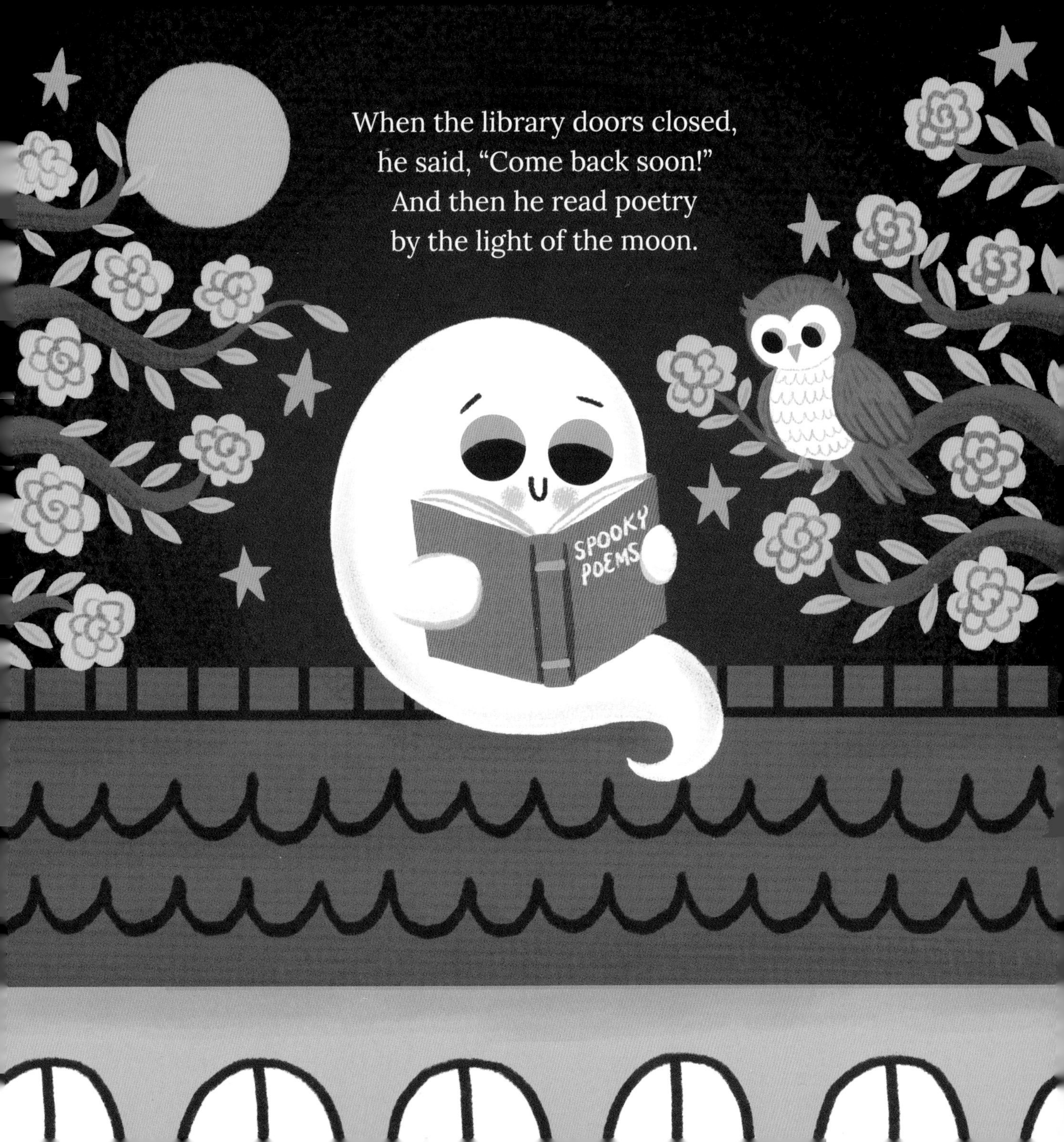
SPOOKY
POEMS

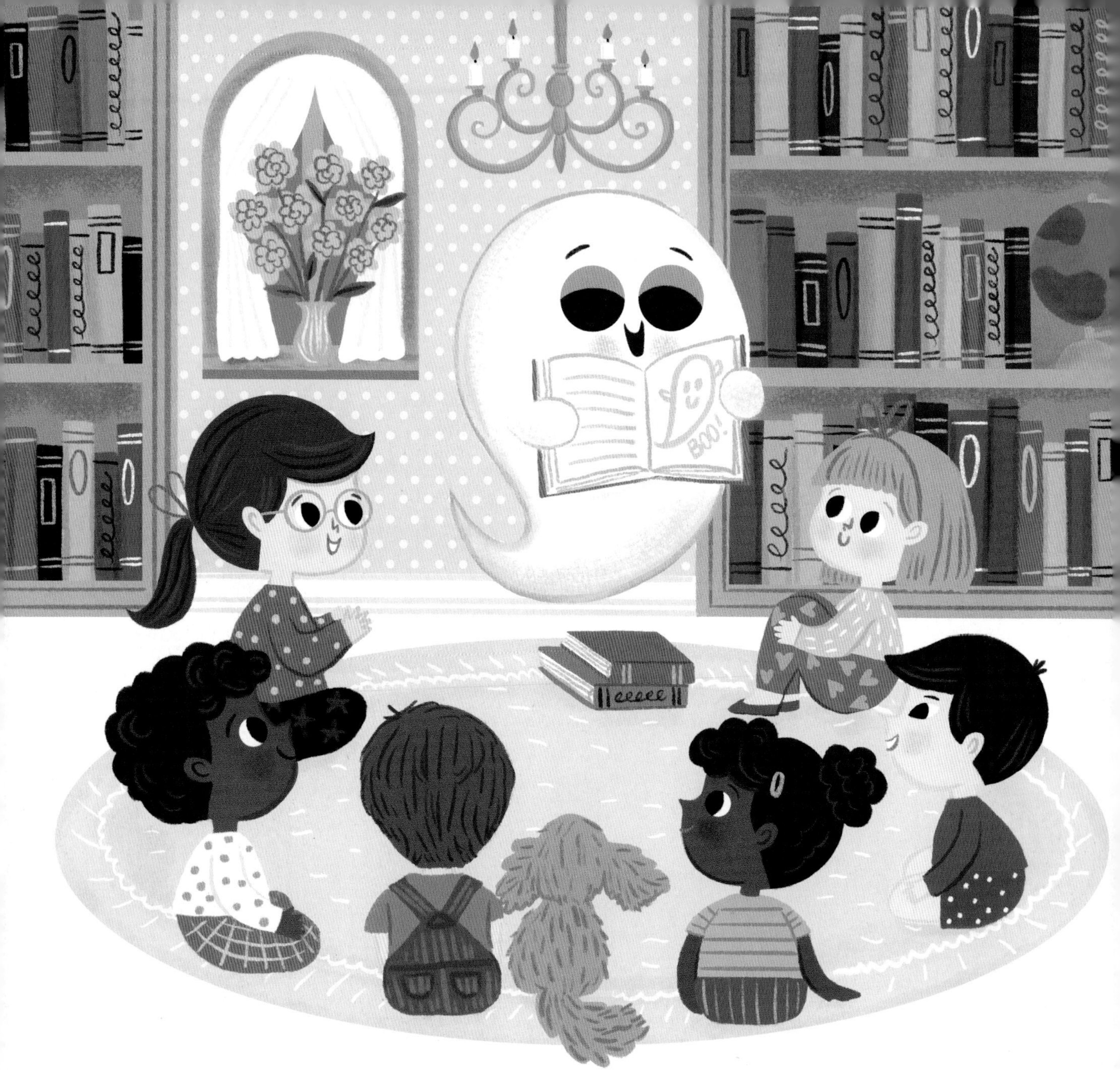
BOO!

Haunting the library is what Boo used to love most,
but now he's a ***reader*** and the best library ghost!

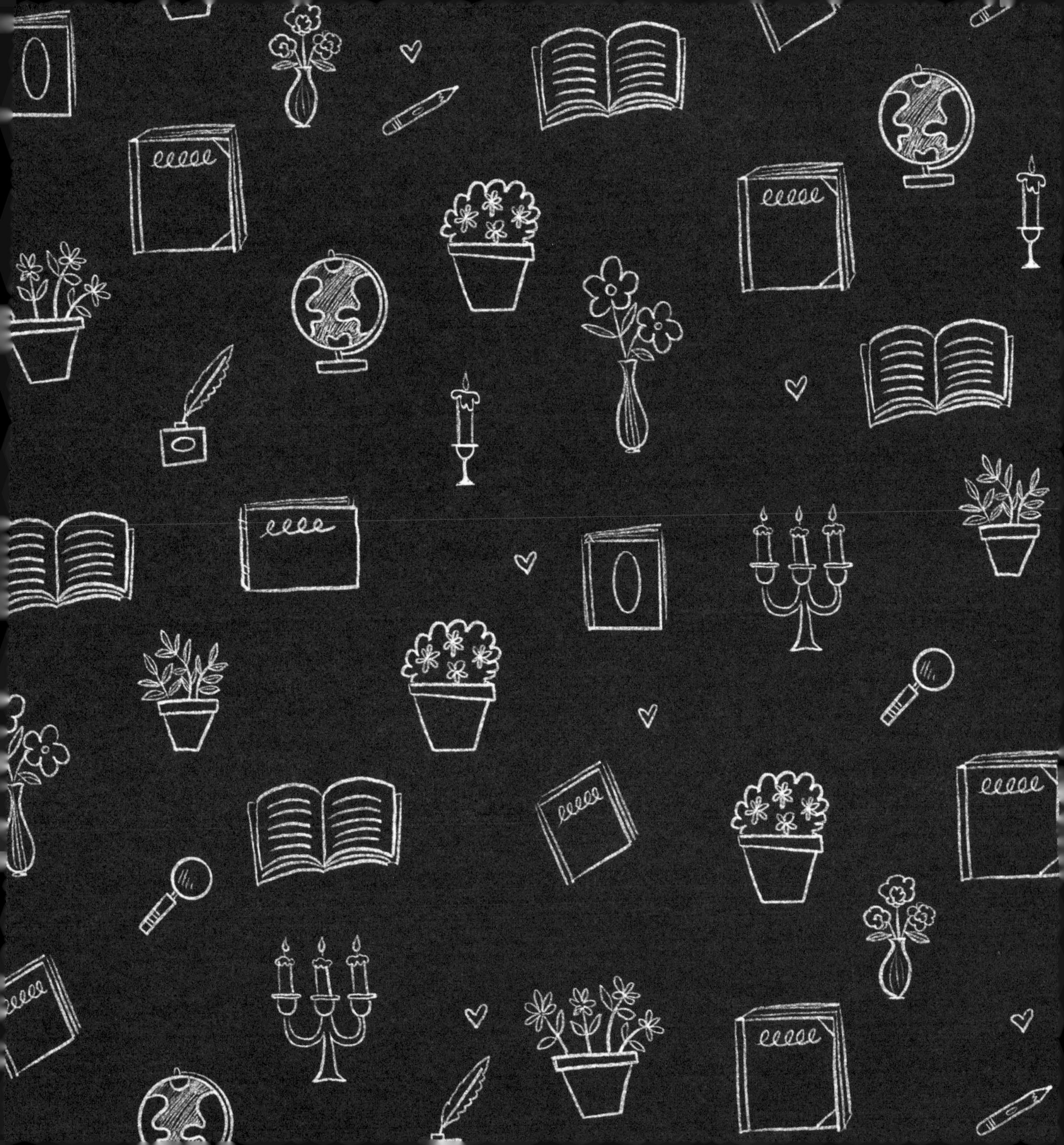

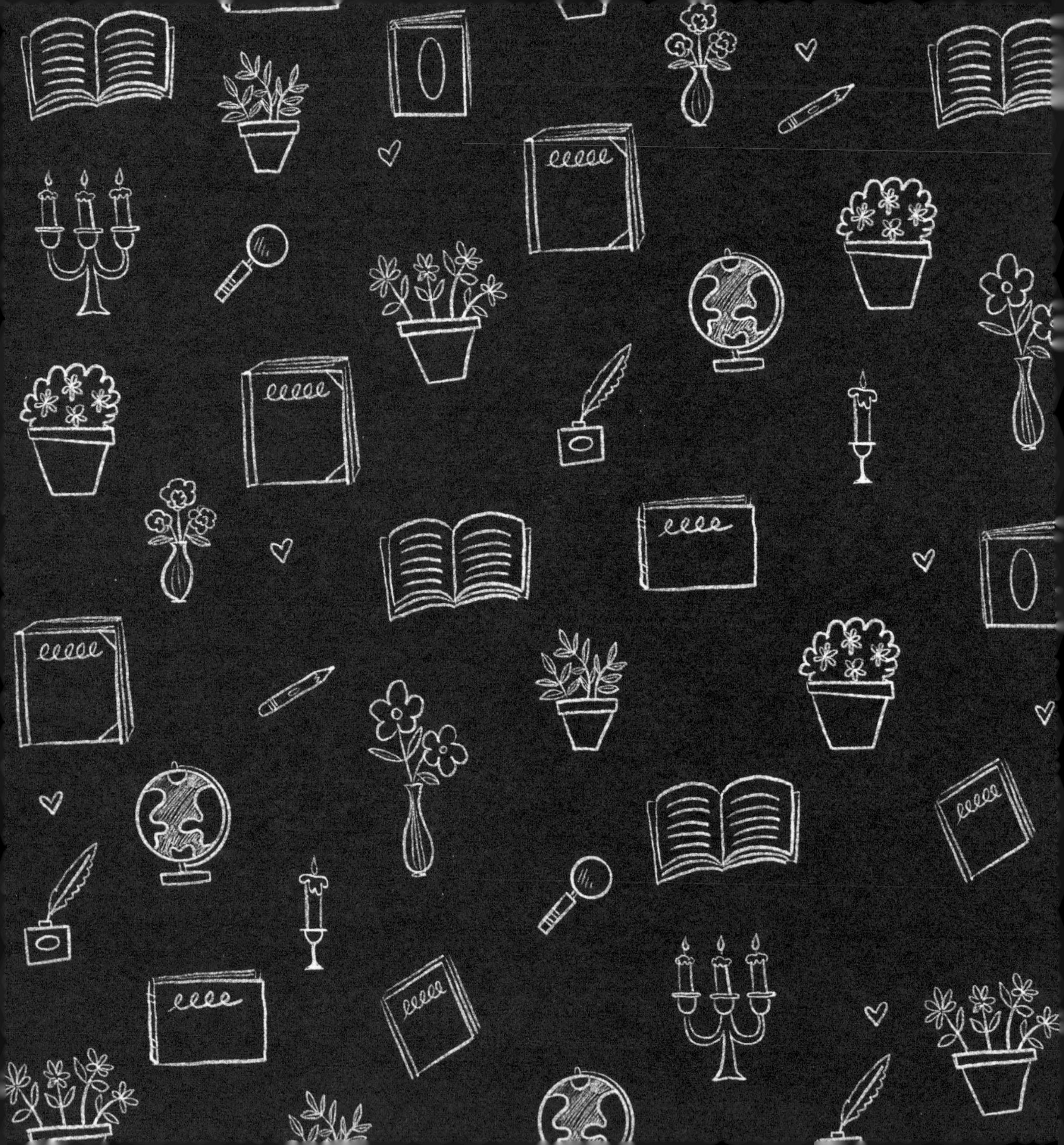